Hide and Seek

Dennis Potter was born in 1935. He studied Politics, Philosophy and Economics at New College, Oxford and edited the review *Isis* from 1958. He worked on *The Sun* for one month, resigning in October 1964: in this year he also stood as a Labour MP.

Dennis Potter's early plays for television included *Vote Vote Vote for Nigel Barton* (1965), *Stand Up for Barton* (1965), *Where the Buffalo Range* (1966), *A Beast With Two Backs* (1968), *Son of Man* (1969), *Traitor* (1971), *Paper Roses* (1971), *Casanova* (1971), *Follow the Yellow Brick Road* (1972), *Only Make Believe* (1973), *Joe's Ark* (1974), *Schmoedipus* (1974), *Late Call* (1975) and *Double Dare* (1976).

Brimstone and Treacle was commissioned in 1975 by the BBC but banned until 1987. The highly acclaimed series *Pennies From Heaven* (1978) won BAFTA's Best Writer's Award and Most Original Production Award, and the film adaptation was nominated for an Academy Award. *Blue Remembered Hills* (1979) won BAFTA's Best Drama Award and two subsequent plays, *Blade on the Feather* and *Cream in My Coffee*, were both nominated for the same award the following year. Two original films, *Dreamchild* (1985) and *Track 29* (1988), were released to great critical acclaim. He adapted for television Scott Fitzgerald's *Tender Is The Night* (1985) and wrote *The Singing Detective* (1986) and *Christabel* (1988).

Dennis Potter is also the author of three novels: *Hide and Seek* (1973), *Ticket to Ride* (1986) and *Blackeyes* (1987) which is also a major television serial, directed by Dennis Potter in 1989.

Married with one son and two daughters, Dennis Potter divides his time between Ross-On-Wye in Herefordshire and London.

ff

DENNIS POTTER

Hide and Seek

faber and faber

LONDON · BOSTON

First published in 1973
by André Deutsch and Quartet Books Limited, London
Reissued in a paperback edition in 1990
by Faber and Faber Limited
3 Queen Square London WCIN 3AU
Reprinted 1990

Printed in Great Britain by
Richard Clay Ltd Bungay Suffolk

A CIP record for this book is available from the British Library
ISBN 0-571-15326-7

For Margaret, my wife

'This dome shone so brightly by the reflection of the costly materials of which it was composed, that he could hardly look toward it. However, as it seemed most to take his attention, he advanced up to the dome.'

James Ridley, *Tales of the Genii*, 1766

PART ONE

INTO THE FOREST

One two three four five six *not yet* seven eight nine *no, no* ten eleven twelve *wait* thirteen fourteen *no!* fifteen *not yet!* sixteen *wait, wait, wait* seventeen *wait!* seventeen seventeen eighteen *no use* nineteen the words were *co-ming!* twent –

'He knows I am trying to escape,' announced Daniel Miller, abruptly.

'Who does? *Who* knows?'

'The Author.'

The two fresh-faced medical students sitting on the big table stopped swinging their legs. Dr Hadley, who had asked the questions, ceased to play with the two-toned ball pen he had been using as a remote muscle of his tongue. A medicine trolley squeaked rodently in the hall outside, where other out-patients sat in clumps of tubular steel chairs neatly arranged according to their various diseases. Daniel, abandoning the effort to count up to a hundred, sensed that brightly coloured biochemicals were jiggling together on the page. Let bards sing now of barbiturates as bright as violets.

'What author?' asked the doctor, unable to stop the rise in his tone.

Daniel sighed, aware that he had attempted to answer all this before, and always to no avail. Those who bothered to listen were astonishingly obtuse or even rude. Sometimes they opened their faces and laughed, taking one step sideways.

'The Author of this Book,' he had replied, twisting away his head a little, almost in shame.

The two silent students looked at each other, eyebrows arching.

'Which book are you talking about, Mr Miller?' persisted Dr Hadley, expressionless. He had taught himself to click out the tip of his ball pen instead of the tip of his tongue.

'*This* Book. The Book I am in. And so the Book you are in. And the Book those two men swinging their legs over there are in.'

When he had got it out Daniel had leaned back in his tubular steel chair with just the suggestion of a smirk on his face. He recognized with some satisfaction that perhaps the most disconcerting thing a character in a novel can do is to announce that he is indeed a character in a novel.

A medicine trolley had squeaked again in the hall outside where the out-patients sat staring at the battleship-grey radiators and the red NO SMOKING notices. Bright bio-chemicals in slippery capsules jiggling on the page, but not the same page.

Daniel knew that he would have to say some more. It was in the plot.

Spreading his swollen hands in a concessionary gesture of exposition he had then explained in a rehearsed tone that he was only as real as the words which made him. He knew, for example, that even such a gesture he was now making was only a pattern in print. But for reasons of caution, or because of the logical and linguistic difficulties of such a contradictory qualification, he did not at that time go on to explain that it

2

was his emancipating conviction (wrestled out of much strenuous mental struggle) that there must also be meaningful senses in which a character, any character, did not wholly belong to his Author. At the very least there should be some untenanted space between the Author's mind and the Author's hand or between the thought thought and the written thought.

Deep, now, in the glooming woods of winter, strapped into this bumping and growling vehicle, Daniel had come to find and to hide in the space where the hitherto omnipotent Author could not quite reach. But he also knew that the malignant and sex-obsessed Creator was trying to close up the gap, the gliding pen dismissing whatever critical intelligence and moral discrimination Daniel aspired to experience.

'He knows, you see. He knows that I know that He knows that I am trying to escape,' he had said yesterday in the curtained-off side room at the old London hospital, trying to place his words carefully in line with whatever was reflecting them down on to page three.

'*He is writing about me!*' Daniel had hissed, leaning in conspiratorially, elbows clunking down on to the doctor's wide desk.

But it had been pointless to try to explain to this goofy idiot and his two white-coated stooges that it was *the Author* who had made him do what he had done and say what he had said. The Author who had stretched out all those women under his joylessly heaving limbs. The Author who made his joints burn, his skin itch, his eyes sting and his head ache. The Author who had lost him his job, lost him his wife, kept him awake at night, made his friends plot against him. Who else could have put the dirty pictures of six variously copulating couples in the inside pocket of his wallet? The Author The Author The Author it was who stiffened his penis as he walked by darkened doorways, who wasted his seed, who . . .

Deeper, now, in the cold woods of Dean, Daniel had come to fight it out with such a sick Creator. Hadley the psychotherapist – who Daniel partly saw as just a minor though characteristically foul-mouthed and impertinent figure in the same turning pages – had not given any sign yesterday that he understood anything that Daniel was trying to say. Instead, the doctor had played with his fluted pen, bared his teeth, scratched his nose, glanced at the two students, scribbled on a pad and asked too many dirty questions. Might as well talk to a grandmother clock.

'I am sick to death,' was the right explanation, 'of this comma-drop in my mind. Tired beyond endurance of the words words dirty words malodorous words stinging at my forehead or stenching at my nostrils just ahead of what I had for too long mistakenly presumed to be my *own* thoughts, my *own* desires. Weary, so weary, of the venomous muttering and whispering and sniggering and finger-pointing of most (if not all) of the other principal characters in His book. Especially, as an educated man, and as a lecturer in liberal studies, especially, as a hard-working Oxford scholarship boy who did very well in later endeavours, especially am I disgusted to the point of retching by the sordid devices and obscene tricks He has employed against me in the narrative ever since the summer night He caused that black haired staring eyed sagging titted narrow hipped red red mouthed tart to suck and dribble at me on the tufty grass in Hyde Park . . . '

But Daniel believed that he was making progress. He was working it out. Most characters in most books and, he realized, all the other characters in this one are totally unable to discern let alone admit the true nature of their common predicament. Only the one theologian he had ever talked to (over a pot of coffee in a hotel lobby) had shown the faintest glimmer of understanding, but even this man had suddenly got up and walked away, looking at the patterns on the carpet. It did not take Daniel much intellectual effort to work out that when people in their distant, unlocatable unease invoked the name of Almighty God they were simply referring to

4

something which is another character in the same Book, even if cunningly constructed so as to share many of the attributes, some of the power and much of the vindictive capriciousness of The Author.

Daniel was working it out, still working it out.

He knew, for instance, that the marginally more subtle or devious of the people he had met did not rise up and shake their fists at the iniquities of a so-called God but chose instead to blame the dislocations and malfunctions of society ('the system', as they called it from under their hair) for their sense of loss or feeling of being manipulated.

As far as Daniel was concerned they were still hanging their harps in the trees and weeping for Zion. In effect, they were objecting to the plot of the Book without even realizing that the Book, let alone the Author, existed. They were fish who did not know about the sea.

Daniel had developed his thesis to the point where he could no longer be so easily misled, and his confidence in this analysis was capable of withstanding the (to him) initially shocking realization that the Author must already by now have written down in some sort of orderly sequence the observation that Daniel had developed his thesis to the point where he could no longer be so easily misled. It made the contest more difficult, but this (elicited by a circuitous question) was the one problem which the sawdust-coloured theologian in the Randolph Hotel had immediately understood and shown to be capable of resolution. See Jeremiah 23, 24.

Naturally, Daniel had not yet worked everything out to his own complete satisfaction. There were many contradictions and difficulties in logic to be untangled. He knew that the struggle would take many pages, much torment, many thousands of words. He was bound to be unsure at this early stage precisely what relationship existed between himself and the Author.

There were times, golden days, when he felt independent,

when he knew that his actions escaped the pen. Ten thousand million blank pages.

More often, though, he could feel the weight of the words on his limbs, he could sense his position on the page and vividly experience the compulsions which dragged him through this or that twist of the plot, up this stairway, down that tunnel, into this bed, ten point on twelve, Garamond.

In recent months Daniel had noticed that he often felt better and upon a few occasions had even been lit up in a swift blaze of exultation after he had remembered and quoted more or less accurately (like Hazlitt) words from other, older and better books. It was as if such an activity soothed the sting at his forehead. Daniel argued that even the tubular-steel Hadleys of this Book would be compelled in plain logic to concede that if he, Daniel, used words other than those originally composed by the Author, if he called in the help of poets and novelists and essayists greater by far and cleaner by far than He, then the Author's tyrannous authority was inevitably weakened. Plagiarism was therefore no piddling offence against private property but, in Daniel's mouth, a venomous act of rebellion. Or blasphemy.

So he now deliberately coaxed up into his mind words from the calm opening of another book. A book in which he was supposed to play no part, pages which had no room for his guilts and fevers. He shifted in the driving seat, sore, and let the words come.

To dwellers in a wood almost every species of tree has its voice as well as its feature: at the passing of the breeze the fir-trees sob and moan no less distinctly than they rock, the holly whistles as it battles with itself, the ash hisses amid its quiverings, the beech rustles while its flat boughs rise and fall . . .

But this time it didn't work. There was no magic in such incantation, refreshing though it could have been to go further Under The Greenwood Tree, listening to the orchestrated trees swaying from another's pen, waiting in present shadow for the good folk with glowing lanterns and buttered vowels to step in soft crunch out of the darkness, hands outstretched to support him.

Daniel had wanted to explain to Hadley that there were some novels in which he would have been happy or even privileged to dwell. He could have given the toothy doctor a list as long as the two swinging legs of the silent, saucer-faced students in the room. But he had by that time admitted to himself that it was impossible for a modern character to infiltrate himself successfully into the landscapes, relationships and serenities of earlier works. He could not jump from one block of pages into another.

'But certainly my own present existence, my own way of life,' he had said calmly enough to the increasingly fretful Hadley, 'is in comparison with characters in earlier works, in works still holding within their spines those cleaner and clearer and infinitely more noble things silently gone out of mind——'

'Works?' interrupted Hadley, trying to locate a key word, or any word.

'Novels. Certainly my own existence – if you will allow me to continue – certainly the way of life which has been and is being – *imposed* – upon me is, thanks to the deficiencies and corruptions and – and – moral sickness of the Author——'

'Which Author?' But Hadley already knew the kind of answer which would come snapping back across the litter on his desk.

'The Author of this Book. This dirty Book.'

Daniel glowered at the two students and then rocked gently in his chair, sucking in his breath as though there was a drinking straw in his mouth.

'The Author,' he said eventually, spitting out the word. 'He is the one. He – arranges things, plots, writes them down, pins me on the – the p . . . page.'

Hadley had waited, determined not to ask another question for a while.

7

'Thanks to *His* spiritual bankruptcy my own actions are – contaminated. I am polluted with the – slime of His creation, the dirt and doubt and disease and despair and and and *obscenity*——'

'Sex,' said Hadley, proffering the word like a lump of sugar. 'You are talking about sex.'

Silence, except for numbers counted in the head.

Daniel clenched his thick hands. Hadley slipped his finger along the silvery flutes of his pen. The two students swung their legs. Then a heavy-footed staff nurse went past the door, jangling a bunch of keys, on her way to cupboards filled with magic.

'Why are those two men swinging their legs?' asked Daniel.

'Take no notice. It doesn't matter,' Hadley had replied, irritated in any case by these two onlookers sitting on the table. They both reminded him of Buster Keaton, lugubrious and hapless, and in the bloody way.

'You are – ah – disturbed or upset by some aspect of sex,' the doctor announced with as much delicacy as time and habit allowed. 'Is that it? Is that what is bothering you?'

Daniel clenched, unclenched. Sausage fingers. He called up the intended satisfactions of fir trees which sob and moan, holly that whistles, hissing ash and rustling beech. But all that came to him then, on the other side of yesterday's desk, was the image of an old elm withered by disease, dead branches flailing the air like Lazarus under his funeral bandages.

And now, too, from the inside of the car, a day and a night away from Hadley and the swinging legs, he realized that the trees out there did not distinguish themselves by their sounds. In the frosty dusk he could just about see the quivering without hearing the hiss, just catch the rise and fall of the boughs without receiving the slightest hint of their rustles. The growling metal box shuts him off, reduces his senses to narrower orbit, diminishes them – except those of pain, which are always transportable, under every sky and at any season.

8

His knee is aching. His eyes are burning. His skin itches.

He is tired and confused after almost four hours of hand-hurt at the wheel. The gloom outside seems to be coming from inside his head: and *that* gloom, he thought he knew, could be followed all the way back or all the way forward along the upward slopes and downward loops of words, words, words, words. Words on a page, on several pages, composed out of the malignant and sex-sodden chaos inside the Author's head.

The malformed shapes outside the car windows also appeared to be shifting about inside his head. Daniel knew they were being imposed upon him. He knew that soon these shapes, these uneasily defined lineaments of dusk, would begin to lack all observable configuration as they moved even more uncompromisingly into the ink-soaked pus of his brain.

'I would be grateful,' he said, almost out loud, 'if you will let me have some more light, you big prick.'

Too truculent!

The trees all around nodded secretively together and then, decisively, closed in towards each other, twig feeling for twig, branch meeting branch, trunks bending slowly with thuggish determination. An old trick of the Author, this, intimidating Daniel with hostile jumps of perspective, inexplicable thickenings of light, and swift spurts of sticky sadness.

'Please let me have some more light,' he said, in a moderate tone.

But the brazen trees were still closing in, preparing to rub their nakedness together, getting ready to snigger in labyrinthine mockery.

'Please!' repeated Daniel, genuinely imploring, the sibilant sticking at his teeth.

Many people at various times had observed that the tall, thin, limping man was talking to himself. They smiled or frowned a little, sidelong glanced or lifted their heads. Ah, poor chap. Oh dear oh dear . . .

9

But Daniel considered that he knew what he was doing. The Author had to be addressed upon occasion, if only in the hope that such prayer might temper the obscenity or vindictiveness of His arbitrary visitations.

Released by sibilant pleading he was able to jab at the oval dashboard array and flick the sidelights on to full beam. A little blue eye opened inside the motor car. Outside, in a wholly theatrical transformation, the crinkled dark walls of tall beech on either side of the rutted, winding and still climbing path glistened in swift sequence before draping themselves in a moving mantle of grotesque shadow like animated illustrations out of a German fairy tale.

'Rumpelstiltskin,' announced Daniel Miller with a shout. 'My name is Rumpelstiltskin!'

The frost hard path skewered sharply off to the right so that as the car turned its lights momentarily swathed a way through the tangle of trees. He just had time to register in a delayed story-book flick a roughly triangular clearing behind the irregular lattice: exactly the sort of remote, half-hidden space in which the sour hobgoblin sang and danced around his evening fire of spitting branches.

Rumpelstiltskin would have triumphed in all his dearest wishes if he had clamped down his tongue, stilled his feet, put out the tell-tale fire and so kept the potent secret of his name.

> *As the crackling of thorns under a pot,*
> *so is the laughter of a fool.*

Fragments of the Bible came easily to Daniel, too easily. And they came in the opposite way from the magic conjured by the hobgoblin: not hay into gold, but gold into hay. Even then, no one and nothing could feed off such hay.

There was no comfort, no communion left in the carved and rearing pulpit of the chapel. No joy singing out from between the floppy red covers of Sankey's Book of Hymns.

No more baskets to fill with the scraps of loaves and little fishes. No radiance behind the alabaster angel.

Gold into hay. Angels into whores. Love into sticky slime. Gentle Jesus meek and mild into an imbecile bleeding and screaming on a cross. Holman Hunt's Light of the World on a picture postcard into fellatio scenes of the same dimensions, hidden. Childhood conviction of God watching and caring into adult certainty of some remote, unseen, unknowable, inescapable Author with evil designs and total power.

'I *can* help you, you know,' Hadley had said the day before, simulating the observed confidence of a television medic, all quiet smile and reassurance.

'You are in the same boat,' Daniel snapped. The same Book, he should have said.

'Do you want to talk about – um – would you like to tell me about it?'

'About what? The Book?'

'No.' Hadley smiled comfortingly. 'Sex.'

Daniel had looked all around the room, seeing very little.

'Do you know what your trouble is?' he said, not quite looking at Hadley. 'You've got a dirty mind.'

'Oh?' The doctor's eyebrows lifted with a professional incredulity. 'Sex is *dirty* is it?'

Daniel had again looked all around the room, seeing less.

'Why are those two men swinging their legs?' he asked, the only thing he could think of saying, the only thing which now seemed important.

'Oh?' The doctor's eyebrows arching like inverted commas. 'Sex is dirty is it?'

Dirty? Dirty?

Daniel had clenched his hands again, almost rejoicing in the pull of the swollen knuckles. He decided that, if he could manage to get away, it was time to go. He heard the question, observed the eyebrows, noticed the swinging legs.

11

The Book was full of eccentrics and lunatics as well as the corrupt and the malicious.

It was time to go.

And now, far away from the squeaking trolley and the impertinent questions, now there are trees everywhere, as far as the headlights can see. But he knew that even this wintering timber was servile, ready to obey the gliding pen, alert to some superior will.

'I would like to see – ah – this book of yours,' Hadley had said just before pushing a National Health prescription across the desk with the air of a man floating a paper aeroplane at a querulous child. 'But we'll talk about that next Thursday. Eleven a.m.'

Daniel screwed his head from side to side, astounded by the stupidity of the remark. If the people in the Book could read the Book they would be people reading in the Book that they were reading in the Book whereas——*no!*

'Thank you,' he mumbled instead, crumpling at the prescription form. 'Thank you thank you thank you thank you . . .'

Hadley, glancing at his oyster-shaped watch, delivered up the usual warning about not eating cheese or Marmite or yeast or broad beans or any fermented thing after taking the shiny capsules.

'Cheese?' Daniel asked.

The word had persuaded him that the controlling malevolence he called the Author was outflanking him at every syllable. He had then become aware that the chairs, the desk, the table and the battleship-grey radiator had taken on (or had been given) an uncomfortable or shifty silence. When *things* begin to get embarrassed, when otherwise innocent desk lamps hang their radiant heads in shame, the time for escape can no longer be postponed.

Daniel tiptoed from the room, watched by at least three pairs of eyes.

> Can any hide himself in secret places that I shall not
>   see him? saith the Lord.
>   Do not I fill heaven and earth?

But he got out through the door before Hadley called him
back. First one and then the other student stopped swinging
dangling legs.

When he reached the carbon monoxide of the street Daniel
sensed, half in fear and half in exultation, that the Author
must have resolved to bring this particular section to an end.

A red double-decker went past, on its way to the terminus.

Home may be where you start from but it was surely the
wrong season of the year and the wrong time of the day for
Daniel to return to the remembered woods of childhood. That
starting place had been green and warm in his later dreams,
the sun dappling on soft moss, the paths proud with foxgloves,
the hosts of trees disorderly benevolent and generously
collusive. He could climb an oak and sit there alone for all of
an hour, secret, safe, and yet as alert as a paradisiac bird.

> Happy those early days! when I
> Shined in my angel infancy
> Before I understood this place
> Appointed for my second race,
> Or taught my soul to fancy aught
> But a white, celestial thought . . .

'Lost,' he said in an incantatory voice. 'Lost.'

But any moment now the headlights should throw halogen
fire on to the squat outline of the old Forestry cottage which
was going to be Daniel's retreat for the next twelve months.
The nominally bleak incantation, therefore, had tinges of
other and brighter colour in it, like mist in malachite. He

knew the cottage could be no more than a thousand or so trees away.

It had been advertised for letting by the Forestry Commission in one of the posh Sunday papers. As soon as Daniel felt that the Author was momentarily out of mindshot the following morning he had telephoned the Crown Offices at Coleford and gabbled out an offer which a steady-voiced man told him to put in writing – preferably after having seen the place.

'I don't need to,' Daniel had insisted. 'I know what it's like.'

He was fairly sure that he remembered the cottage, nearly three miles along a track into the woods, close by an abandoned quarry and a little further from a small coal-mine once worked by four of his distant cousins. The mine had its tunnel driven into the side of a steep bank, making the hill look as though it had a toothless mouth. Four or five hundred yards from the black hole the trees on the slope had sagged towards each other, disturbed by the human moles working beneath their long roots.

The advertisement, with its severely abbreviated detail, had provoked the disconcertingly potent ache of nostalgia in him far more swiftly than if he had come across a more eloquent or decorative celebration of his native Forest of Dean. Green, celestial thought, solidified in memory.

TO LET unf. on ann. lease, renewable. Isolated, unmodernized but sound cottage Forest of Dean. 3 rooms. K. No tel. No elec. Built 1735. Details, map, tenders etc. Crown Commission Office, Coleford, Glos.

Many townspeople came and looked at it, tapped the walls, stamped on the floor, opened and shut the doors, walked all round it making sensible-sounding noises and squashed their noses against the windows. But the rooms were to any eye miserably small, labourer sized, woodchopper high. The ceilings were bumpy and sloped suspiciously towards windows not much bigger and not much brighter than family bibles.

In the end, nobody else had wanted the place. Perhaps nobody else had quite the same need.

After six weeks and seventeen tentative approaches the only serious tender came from Daniel.

He had offered a paltry £2 a week for the one-time woodman's home, sane enough in this, at least, to calculate safety to the nearest new penny piece. He hoped – in the canny deftness of an old confidence – that his offer would be considered high enough to purchase the peace and healing seclusion he knew he needed if he was ever to put down a decade of pain and disappointment and finish the critical biography of Samuel Taylor Coleridge which he had begun with such book-gutting zest in his last year at Oxford, two years before his marriage.

Bliss was it in *that* dawn, too.

Daniel had explained to his wife Lucy, when she last visited him, that he could live in brave and glorious isolation for a whole year in the Forest of Dean for less than the cost of two months rent of his (once *their*) tatty, paint-peeling so-called mansion block flat in tatty, paint-peeling so-called Shepherd's Bush.

'Put like that . . .' she began.

He swirled on to compare seven weeks in a flat filled with miserable happenings suspended heavily above traffic snarl, pavement noises, an eel-and-pie shop, an automatic laundry, a tobacconist's and a hardware store to a whole year, to all four seasons, in an eighteenth century woodcutter's cottage set down as though by natural right among old trees and potentially rediscoverable memories. How – he demanded, before falling silent – how could any sane person doubt where the advantage lay?

'It seems a very good idea in theory,' said Lucy, warily, watching him all the while.

His forehead was pressed against the smudged window pane, his swollen hands clenching like banana bunches into his sides, his feet turning uncertainly inwards as though trying to keep on some hidden tightrope.

'Bitch!' a word splattering on the glass, an aerosol expletive.

Lucy sighed and turned to go.

Forehead back against cool window he churned love and hate in his head, mixing in and out of trees, remembered trees, headlight blazing trees and other, darker foliage. A woman in white boots lit a rolled newspaper. An Italian showed him a tobacco tin filled with chunky rings. A boy cried alone in the bracken.

Lucy sighing, turning to go, too far from the old cry.

Forehead against glass he knew she would not wake by his side, knew she could not see the pictures in his head, the diseased elm at his groin, the pen on the page . . . the dead bracken, brown as sin.

'Bitch!' he had shouted.

Lucy had sighed and turned to go, unknowingly waist-high in innocent green fern.

'Lucy,' he said, turning away from the window, 'I am sorry. I don't want to say words like that. I don't *want* to abuse you. Lucy?'

She stood still, examining him, her green eyes brimming.

He hung his head and turned back to the window. But there was nothing to see, nothing but what had happened and had been written down. And none of it could be erased, not by one jot nor tittle.

'Lucy,' he whispered, looking out of the hole. 'It wasn't me. I didn't say that. It wasn't *really* me . . .'

She stepped back, defensively.

This 'really not me' bit terrified her. He had used the expression more and more in the months before their break, and she had grown to recognize the awe in his face as the words were formulated. She could feel his helplessness, sense his desire to disown some deed or substance within himself, but by now she also knew the danger of it, the violence, the sickness. It could happen that he would leap across the room at her, arms flailing, knocking her to the floor. Then he would pick or pull her up, crying, disclaiming responsibility. 'Really not me.'

Once – and only once – he had spoken to her of the Author. At first she had thought he was talking about God, which is understandably an embarrassing subject between married couples. But when taxed about it he had gone quiet, face as pale as bone china, eyes burning in his head like reflector glass. Then his fist had flung out again, obscenities in his mouth.

Stepping back, defensively, she realized when he again whirled round from the window that some such violence was boiling up as before.

'Get back!' she hissed.

'Bitch!' stepping towards her. 'Dirty fucking whore!'

'Daniel! No!'

The car lights suddenly isolated the frightened and alien eyes of a fox in the woods. Sly, slinking creature, thief in the night. The animal slunk off the page, leaving him only the luminous impression of other eyes, human eyes, pleading eyes.

'Please . . . !' he released the call again.

Where, oh where, was his new haven-to-be? Why was it taking so long to get along this track? Could he have gone right by the cottage while unthinkingly looking for the beacon of a lighted window?

The wilder thought came like the fox: has He moved things again? Does the cottage really exist at all, even on foundations of words?

He reassured himself. The old building would be dark now, of course, barely discernible from the lower trees, thick stumps or scattered clumps of shrub. It would be just another outcrop, its outline so old and worn, so perfectly in place, that one could go past it in the same way he was now going past these trees.

The car lurched over a fallen branch, jarring his body and making him cry out in a swift gust of animal panic.

'Rumpelstiltskin,' he then said, slowly, trying to calm himself by reverting to a childhood incantation less verbose than prayer. 'My name is Rumpelstiltskin.'

As a child Daniel had never liked being alone in these endless woods when the sun had impaled itself upon the spiked and jagged horizon. Drying twigs snapped, owls hooted, foxgloves coughed, fitful moonlight splashed weirdly suggestive patterns through the bars of the branches. Small animals without souls rustled in the undergrowth or, trapped out of cover, suddenly screamed as beak, claw and flutter fell upon them.

All of the older Foresters told soft-voiced tales about strange shapes, lost figures, inexplicable cries in these woods. Daniel's father needed four or five pints of scrumpy cider before he would launch on one such yarn, that of the woman walking by the chestnuts one month after she had been buried.

Daniel could almost catch that voice again, and with it the face, the stance, the rheumy eyes and the air of perpetual apology which had hung about him like an odour. A miner with his head slightly tilted as though forever listening for the creak in the pit prop, the ache in the timber, which was the faint prelude to a roof fall.

The son bumped up and down again in the driving seat, memory shaking at him, hard. The path was narrowing and becoming even more rutted with frozen ripples of earth, dwindling now into what seemed a waiting oblivion where there were no more memories, no more choices. The old building itself was likely to be just another of those chimeras of the woodland which made all Foresters, at heart, superstitious and God-ridden. They grew up with the same ambivalent attitude to the surrounding miles of trees that fishermen had for the sea.

Sweating slightly despite the cold Daniel, a Forester again, dropped from a cautious second to an even more circumspect first gear. The vehicle was now trundling along at little more than walking pace.

The Forest had slowed down. The trees were more rooted. The sky was pitch to his thoughts. Looking, still looking, for the old cottage, childhood itself came out of the ragged black. He put it down, pushed it away.

Where is it! Where is it!

Where?

Each bare tree, gesticulating stiffly on either side of the track, refused to pull back and show. Instead, they reminded him, demanded of him, the admission that in his thirty-five years he had achieved little more than the black art to dispense a several sin to every sense. One hundred and fifty-six prostitutes and a wife with lucid green eyes sobbing on a settee with a stinging red weal on half her once gentle face. One hundred and fifty-six whores and a bottle of pretty capsules which do not mix with cheese or broad beans or any fermenting thing.

Daniel's left knee was aching more insistently now, an elongating bubble of pain moving slowly through the joint like a rotting memory caught in ligament. There were times, like now, when he feared that the Author was slowly pumping bad air into him, for most of his joints were swollen. If it kept on like this, pump pump, he would fill up like a balloon, swell up until, unanchored, he would float away into the illiterate void above the schematic trees.

A passing wood pigeon would plunge in a trailing claw and let out all the stinking gas. The poor, puckering corpse would fall back again into the branches beneath. He would be caught there like a used French Letter, dribbling out rancid juices, accumulated residues of A Nice Time Darling . . .

'Throw it in the bin, love.'

'Come back in nine months time and I'll have a little something for you, eh?'

'Get on with it! Push! *Push!*'

Sequences of such words elongated into the bubble elongating itself in his knee joint, his fingers, his shoulder, his jaw.

'Throw it in the bin!'

'Oh?' as Hadley's eyebrows lifted, 'Sex is *dirty* is it?'

Daniel looked all around the Forest, seeing everything.

Rain: how long had it been raining? Here, in the depths, heavy rain often sounded like a chorus of old women muttering and murmuring and spitting amongst themselves in hag malice. A small tree, broken in a previous storm, bent down over the path in the posture of an old witch. Bony fingers scraped possessively at the roof of the car. Daniel's shudder went right through to the gingerbread wheels.

Looking, still looking, for the old cottage, childhood itself came out of the ragged black. He could not put it down, could not push it away.

Where is it? Where is it? Where?

No cartographer can trace on any known map the place where we were born and bred. Unlocatable is that lost land where we first hear someone calling our name. Gone is the place where we learn to speak and read and laugh and cry (or, worse, not to cry), gone like trees walking. The oval blob as distant as any planet leans in with rattling things, strange noises, an unrecognized smile, a blob which slowly becomes a face, a dimension, a recognized frown. The face becomes a person, and then there are several, oddly communicating persons teetering upright and loud and giant in a clock-ticking cavern. A house, a home.

And the house, longtime centre of all, grows grey and green around itself, breathes changing banks of cloud above itself, catches songs, whistles, shouts, tastes, coughs and whispers and bed-creaks within itself. Half remembered half dreams conjuring shapes too resonant, too private to be easily put into public and adult words.

Looking for the old cottage in the woods Daniel had yet to realize that he was seeking just such an impossible place, the abandoned place. But even if he had not so far in sickness nor in sanity acknowledged that the sense of such loss is part of our metabolism, an ache never to be assuaged, he had nevertheless already begun to work out that this loss necessarily sets up some of the outer boundaries of literary endeavour.

And so somewhere in the yet merciful, God-still eye of his word-blown tornado there was the faintest configuration of rational hope, the flimsiest lineament of the sacred reason that engages itself in meaningful search. He was in combat at last.

Daniel knew that the Author knew that he was bumping up and down in a swollen, sweaty fear along this narrowing, frost-hardened track. But Daniel also sensed that the Author might well get *lost* here. He had argued (to or with himself) that the Author would for once be placed in a situation where He might fail to be in total command of the landscape and its figures. Here, in this river-bounded and hilly Forest, shimmering in memory, Daniel must once have – he searched the books – felt through all this fleshly dress the bright shoots of everlastingness. Other powers were here, too, impregnating memory with a holier seed, another *He*:

> When yet I had not walked above
> A mile, or two, from my first Love,
> And looking back, at that short space,
> Could see a glimpse of His bright face . . .

'He knows that I know that He knows I am trying to escape,' Daniel had said yesterday in the curtained-off room in the hospital, mentally trying to hold a mirror against a mirror.

Aged seven, he had examined the bottle of Camp Coffee on the kitchen table, mentally trying to hold a label against a label, his small white face trying too hard to understand eternity.

'What's the matter with you!' his mother, accusing, clearing away plates, cups and saucers with an obtrusively busy chink-chink.

'This bottle. The label on this bottle.'

His mother sighed: questions, questions. She had produced a child who asked too much and yet spoke too little, who did not want to go out to play with the three boys next door and who apparently went off into the woods *by himself*.

'I'm trying to clear up.'

'Mum! Look at the label on this coffee!'

'Oh for Christ's sake!'

But she looked. There was always an urgency or even a thrill of awe about his demands which compelled at least the outward forms of attention, from parent or teacher or man sitting in the sun on the low wall outside the pub, swinging his legs, swinging . . .

Together, without speaking, mother and child examined the pretty label.

'What's the matter with it, then?' she asked at last, quite willing to be surprised by something she had failed to see.

Daniel let out his breath in a slow, sad hiss.

'What's up with it!' she said, much more sharply, reacting to his disappointment.

The boy looked up at her, puzzled by such tones, and then explained in the irritating voice of an adult addressing a child that on the label of the bottle there was a big Scottish man in a kilt sitting outside a tent with a flag and being brought some coffee on a tray by a brown man in a turban.

'He's a servant,' she said, citizen of an Imperial power.

Daniel flapped his hand in annoyance, pointing out in quicker speech that the tray being carried by the brown man had a bottle of Camp Coffee on it. And the bottle on the tray had a label – *see!* – on which there was the same big Scottish man in a kilt sitting outside the same tent with the same flag being brought the same coffee on the same tray by the same brown man in a turban. And – quicker still – the brown man in a turban on the label on the bottle in the label was carrying a tray with a bottle with a label on which you could just see again a big Scottish man in a kilt sitting outside a tent being brought some coffee on a tray by a brown man in a turban.

Words almost out of control, the boy was delving down into the scarcely discernible third and indecipherable fourth layer before his mother picked up the remaining cup and saucer and clanked them together in the washing-up bowl.

'It goes on and on,' Daniel raised his voice, trying to call her back. 'It goes on and on for ever and ever and ever.'

'It's only a bloody picture!'

Elbows hard on the table, eyes fixed on the high shouldered bottle, he tried to work out how the Indian and the Scot could ever not be haunted by themselves. And then, suddenly, he had a picture of himself, elbows on the table, looking at the bottle, a picture which had narrowed within it the picture of himself, elbows on the table, looking at the bottle, within which he again sat elbows hard on the same but smaller table . . . while in each diminishing leap there remained the label showing a big Scottish man in a kilt sitting outside a tent with a flag and being brought some coffee on a tray by a brown man in a turban.

Thoughts almost out of control, the boy was delving down into the scarcely discernible third and indecipherable fourth and incomprehensible fifth layer before his recurring mother, placed backwards, picked up the remaining cup and saucer and clanked them together in the washing-up bowl, washing-up bowl, bowl, bowl.

'It goes on and on,' Daniel raised his voice, in a thrill of terror. 'It goes on and on for ever and ever and ever.'

'It's only a bloody picture!'

The boy slowly rolled his head from side to side, trying to absorb the shock.

'It goes on,' he insisted, 'on and on and on and on and on and——'

'Shut up!' she shouted, turning on the tap, swishing away the words.

'On and on and on and on and on——' he was still chanting when she had turned the water off, the sounds in his mouth as mechanical as tiny pistons.

'Danny!'

'On and on and on and on . . .'

'Danny! Stop it!'

'And on and on.' The words ended, power switched off, mouth clamping shut.

They both waited, she in the doorway, dishcloth in her hand, he at the table. One, two, three, four, five, six. Then he began to scream.

'Daniel!'

Trapped in halls of mirror, tunnels of words, he continued to scream. He screamed until she hit him in panic, hard, across the face, her hand slippery with soap.

'Next time,' she said, her eyes stinging, her hand stinging, 'I'm buying some bloody Bev!' Another bottle of coffee essence with added chicory but without premature intimations of immortality.

'Next time,' she had said, so long ago, 'I'm buying some bloody Bev!'

On and on and on: the still kinking, coldly kicking, still shrinking track itself had become endless, repeating the same greys and browns, back to sights and sounds and moods that must surely once have occupied real space in real time.

The label on a sticky bottle. A throaty tick-h tock-h tick-h tock-h, almost conversational, of a chipped grandmother clock on a rose-patterned wall, its tarnished pendulum perpetually on the move behind the little glass window of a resonant cage.

On and on and on: the still kinking, coldly kicking, still shrinking track had become endless, repeating the same trees, the same eyes of the same fox, the used flesh behind the used branches, transmitting the same bumps . . .

A blackbird's egg breaking in his mouth. A witty mongrel barking at dusk, clanking a chain. Metal rings in a tobacco tin. And the voices of the dead, too, all but alive, calling back across the shimmery pool before yet another, perhaps more merciful torrent swept them away in a cataract of dismissal to allow a different rivulet to leak different pictures and different voices into what must have been an adjacent pool, fringed by nerves of similar hue.

The label on a sticky bottle . . . ?

The flag on the tent on the label in the trees had a slogan or something written on it. He strained at this moment to bring it back, to fish the flag up out of that sudden pool between the beeches. But the words on the flag, hovering almost alphabetically on the tip of his nerve, refused to surface and shape themselves. He inadvertently caught instead his mother's thin voice, then lost that too. A cup chinked in a bowl, then was gone. A dog barked at dusk. A chain clanked. A silicosis cough rattled tin-tacks in a man's chest and some black phlegm sizzled on the hot bars of the grate. Grancher!

Roses on the wall. The pendulum swinging to the left, to the right. Tick-h tock-h. There was something rattling in the car. Tick-h tock-h came glinting dully up at the windscreen, blobbing and splattering with speed-worried globules of rain. Metal rings in a tobacco tin.

Whose memories are these?

The unexpectedly italicized question flew up at Daniel with the swift, terrified flutter of a yellowhammer startled in a gorsebush. Perhaps this was the way lucidity leapt up in the insane or madness sprang wild in the lucid, yellow flash of livid flight out of yellow flowers dancing on thorns.

Whose memories?

Daniel allowed the bird to recede twittering into the haze and addressed himself as calmly as he could to the question. There was hope and there was fear in the alternative answers. He had to be sure he knew what was going on at this point in the text.

If the memories so recently on the page belonged to Daniel, only to Daniel, then surely they preceded the intervention of the Author? If (Daniel reasoned) *if* he could remember things like the coffee bottle and the blue egg breaking in his mouth, if he could virtually occupy again moments of time or segments of place which had happened before the Author had made him up, then surely

YOU HAVE MADE THE AUTHOR UP. YOU ARE THE AUTHOR.

The capitals flashed like a neon sign unexpectedly switched on at the top of a dark warehouse in the middle of an abandoned city. They were grotesquely bright and shocking.

'You have made the author up,' Hadley had insisted the day before. 'You are the author.'

TAKE YOUR TABLETS.

The capitals again. The shudder again. Lucy sighing again, turning to go. Hadley lifting his eyebrows. A soapy hand smacking into his face.

TAKE YOUR TABLETS.

He fought for a while with the steering wheel, hoping it was a real steering wheel, waiting for the admonition to burn away. He sensed that the capitals, which came in intermittent stings totally unlike the jabs of pain afflicting all other parts of the body, would eventually retreat back into the lower-case typography within which, indisputably, he existed.

An awkward, evasive bend was once again being negotiated

in this treescaped passage, foot barely touching the tiny accelerator pedal, hands still determinedly clinging to the slithering steering wheel.

Take your tablets.

He had managed it. He had straightened out into the lower-case and was now able, through a sheen of sweat, to acknowledge once more the superb cunning of the Author. Persistently, diabolically, the Author succeeded in tricking him into almost denying what all the other less resilient characters had been deluded into denying within the very same pages which continued to set out as clear as printers' ink the multitudes of ways in which he, Daniel Miller, was being manipulated and corrupted. Daniel reasserted to himself that the Author did indeed exist.

So those memories hinted at on preceding pages were *not* his memories at all, except in the same intimidating way in which all the other words had been put together. Any author was duty bound to give his characters a past, unless they were mere bystanders caught out of the corner of the eye, simple decorations of the text.

But those memories were surely in some manner not yet understood really his own memories? Was this not why he was returning to this place? Were they not part of his weapons in the fight against cunning diabolism? Did they not hint at webs or traps within which the Author would be held at bay and his own dignities re-claimed?

Daniel fixed his mind on the easier revelation that the Author had not intervened or interceded or 'made him up' at one particular point in his life. There had simply been one particular moment when the bundle of impressions, premonitions, hints, fears and insights had flared together in a sizzle of revelation to tell him that he, Daniel, was a character in a novel. A novel, moreover, from which he had every reason, every righteous impulse, to try to escape.

A dirty book, peopled with foul creatures, stained flesh,

27

dirty pictures, faithless women with rotting cunts, sucking mouths. Yes, a dirty book, yes, yes, rolling him in its filth, spelling him out, spilling him out, in long lines of pornographic despair, rubbery despond, triste post coitum ... degenerate paragraphs, obscene posturings, fleeting trees hiding silky thighs and rosily tender nipples.

He sucked in his breath and felt the deadly tingle at his loins, the sudden lift of stiffening sinew, the familiar prelude to the familiar betrayal.

In his pocket – he tried to push away the thought – in his pocket there was a booklet folded – push it away – in his pocket because he had not destroyed it there were pictures coldly made out of his old fevers. He could not push them away.

Again, the sticky dampness at him, Daniel tried and tried to fix his mind on the revelation that the Author had not intervened or interceded or 'made him up' at any one particular point in his life. This meant – and the erection was subsiding – this surely meant that it left open the possibility that Daniel had once had a life and could again *find* a life in which the Author *was not there*.

Triumphantly, Daniel reaffirmed that this search for emancipation was the reason for the journey. He must not allow himself to be deflected from this objective, no matter how clever or sustained the wiles of the demon he was attempting to cast aside. He must be more alert than he had ever been before, prepared for every kind of assault, every sly infiltration. The dead or sleeping foliage out there in the headlights would not protect him, for it was only a different form of invention.

The frost hard path skewered sharply off to the right so that as the car turned its lights momentarily swathed a way through the tangle of trees. He just had time to register in a delayed story-book flick a roughly triangular clearing behind the irregular lattice: exactly the sort of remote, half-hidden space in which a sour hobgoblin sang and danced round his evening fire of spitting branches.

But he had seen this before. He had been on that page.

Where was he? Why were the trees the same? Why was the path repeating itself in every tiny detail, every kink and twist, every fallen branch, every pattern of its ridges and rills?

The landscape was not neutral in this battle. It was being played with. *He* was being played with. And now there was a totally meaningless picture in his head, unrelated to anything else in all the paragraphs he had endured: a white silhouette on dark purple, deep purple, shaped like a sailing ship with nine diagrammatic sails, bobbing up and down.

There was rain on the windscreen. He was finding it difficult to see, but what he could see he had surely seen before.

But the beech trees were so close that it was dangerous to drive between them. They had the worn hide of circus elephants and only had to move in clumsy malice or a worse boredom to crush his little metal box. He wondered with an almost insane indifference when he would be allowed to switch on the windscreen wipers.

Daniel calmly watched nine white sails drift off into a diminishing patch of purple. He could no longer be sure that his hands were still clamped to the steering wheel. He was conscious of little except extreme tiredness and a sense of defeat. There was nothing and nobody to call upon, and although he was now convinced that the accumulating paragraphs had ensured that he had long since missed the cottage (if it was ever there) Daniel lacked the energy or the motive to turn back. The patch of purple was now no more than a mere speck, a spot on the edge of his mind, waiting to deepen into black.

He acknowledged without rancour the certainty that he would drive on and on for ever (or, more accurately, be driven on) until the car was absorbed into that blackness. Memory fades into treescape, living tissue into diseased elm,

29

skin into beech bark, madness to nightfall, movement into paralysis, desire into bracken, coldly powdering, and physical pain into the meshing, mashing oblivion of owl-hoot and guilt and rustle and animal scream and dead vegetation, all that remained of his personal identity.

Daniel prepared to abandon himself.

'It goes on and on,' said an impossibly distant voice, unlarynxed. 'It goes on and on for ever and ever and ever and ever.'

'It's only a bloody picture!'

But even as he abandoned himself, at the very edge of mindless oblivion, the vague outline of a song came unbidden to his brain. Before the words of it came, before the tune even, he stirred out of total apathy back into more positive unease: a new unease, or an old one, soft in form, insidious, the kind he had associated with the tune since he had been an infant. The speck of purple expanded again. Memory at the deepest level was struggling to reassert itself, and seconds later, as the path once more spiralled, the words bumped out and arranged themselves in sequence out of the furthest recesses of his being.

> When the deep purple falls
> Over sleepy garden walls
> And the stars begin to flicker in the sky
> Through the mists of memory
> You wander back to me . . .

Reassembled, a real memory, an impulse back to a kind of coherence. The unbidden act turned into a mode of experience, a willed assertion. The trees separated out again, mere rooted things.

> When the deep purple falls
> Over sleepy garden walls.

These words were almost certainly the longest string of

awkward syllables that he had first wound into a complete segment during his early childhood. They came only a little later than Little Bo Peep and one for the master, one for the dame and what a good boy am I, am I.

The song must have been popular in the summer which ended with the declaration of war against Hitler's Germany. It merged at points into the wail of siren or more raucous lyrics about hanging washing on the Siegfried Line. But it also had within the schmaltzy gentleness of its rhythms a lot of the lost grace people meant or thought they meant when they said 'before the war, we——'.

Daniel followed the words back, as far as they would take him, past splattered windscreen, sullen timber, beyond this present track, a needle biting into a groove, a little dog listening at a horn loudspeaker, a woman burning a newpaper, voices out of the air, sounds across an ocean.

He had been left alone in the house on the gold-figured afternoon of his fourth birthday. The song had already been played twice on the kennel-shaped wireless which stood on the parlour windowsill. Bing Crosby – or perhaps Al Bowlly, foggy voiced romantic, soon to be slaughtered. Syncopated sounds hissing and crackling into a room now magic with birthday flutters – there were nine or ten coloured cards stacked closely together on the ledge above the empty grate, gaudy messages shining out between a chunky brass figure of three monkeys, hearing, seeing, speaking no evil and, on the other side of the shelf, a demure alabaster lady with some splotched flowers in her little hand.

The third time the song came from the wireless something about the opening bars – or maybe the simulated urgency in the voice of the announcer – caught at the boy's attention, just as he was carefully putting one blue brick on top of a column of red ones. Birthday bricks, still with a glossy sheen.

Daniel listened, head on one side, tongue slowly coming out. Before the song had finished he pushed over the pile of wooden bricks, violently. But he did it without knowing why he wanted to and without knowing why he was glad his mother was out on the well-stones, unable to see him now.

Curled up in bed that night with his knees almost touching his chin he heard the wireless song again, drifting up the stairs, bass notes exaggerated into a monotonous thump, thump. The words were distinct enough, though: weird words droning insidiously into a young mind floating on a nine-sailed ship into the ocean of sleep, the other world he had already come to cherish.

When the deep purple falls
Over sleepy garden walls——

He woke up later that night in a damp bed, calling for a candle. Again and again on the wildly sloping deck, under the flapping white sails, he had been trying to make the last brick stay securely on top of all the others. Always it fell, changing shape, permanently unstable, never fitting, incapable of balance and lacking any response. Waves of deepest purple sucked and swirled at the birthday brick.

Daniel knew very well what Purple was. A colour. As he called for the candle he also called for the word to remain a colour, just a colour. But that call he did not or could not attempt to put into sound.

A colour. Purple was a colour, a colour, nothing but a colour. A chair was a chair, a tree was a tree, an eye was an eye, a brick was a brick, a dog was a dog, a colour was a colour.

But he knew, this boy who could now count up to twenty, he knew that on this day and in this night he could not make sense out of the way the word for the colour was used in the song.

How could a colour fall over a wall? And if walls were sleepy, did they go to sleep, did they *wake up*? What were walls like when they were awake? Perhaps they moved, all the stones together, shifting about on the edges of the garden, breaking up spiders and earwigs, clumping towards the cabbages.

'When the deep purple falls——': one, two, three, four, five, six, *Mum! Mum!* seven, eight, nine, *Mum!*, ten, ten, ten. The only possible conclusion was that the words of the song, mixing up purple and mist and stars and sleepy walls and someone coming back from somewhere, were really about something else. The words meant more than they said, and the words did not mean what they did say. Words were not the same sort of things as chairs, trees, eyes, bricks, dogs and colours?

This was an agitating new concept for the boy in his bed. He stopped calling, he stopped counting and he lay as still as he could, holding his breath, working his mind. Things had been happening in the house, incomprehensible things, and he began now to try to put them together, brick upon brick. But always, always the last brick would not stay in place. Always the pile clattered to the ground, the song coming out of the wireless, his mother standing outside on the well-stones, red marks on her neck, turning purple . . .

Deep purple falling – words had not until that moment existed in any separate way for Daniel. They did not threaten unless they were threatening, explicitly, as with the promise of a clout round the ear. But the song hinted at words with disguises in them or on them, words which behaved like faces, words too complex, the thing grown-ups whispered about together, heads leaning in towards each other as though he was not or should not be in the room.

Deep purple: it wasn't a colour, it wasn't a thing.

But Daniel was later (and now, again) to remember the feel and fear of this strange purple, drooping over the old wall by the coal-shed, drifting above the heavy wooden lid on the well, gathering at his mother's white throat, or waiting shapelessly at night at the bottom of the bed, coiling up in the whirls and whorls of the dark chest of drawers.

A dog barked outside, frantic, clanking the chain. Every nameless thing, every strange event in the household, every sidelong glance, every hiss of speech heard from the distance of another room, all these were absorbed by a creeping seep of purple. He could smell it, a rotting bloom.

Deep purple, the terrifying deep stain of more than thirty years before, he now tried to call by other names or identify by other means. Anxiety was not a colour, not a thing. Guilt was not a colour, not a thing. Carefully putting one blue brick on top of a column of red ones, one new thought on top of the heap of old ones, he could still be transfigured.

He must not find the one hundred and fifty seventh prostitute in these, his native woods. Everything would fall down, a clatter of bone.

But deep purple – he had only to turn his head too quickly to see the suggestion or the aftermath of it receding down a flaking corridor, or to hear it in the creak of bed springs, in the laughter from the other side of the partition, or to sense it in the lighted oblongs jumping up a street, in figures drooping by the window, in spurts from his loins, in birds falling in a black flutter from the air.

Yes, it waited behind closed doors or opened thighs. It clutched hold in the pauses between words. In those sidelong glances, those endless whispers, those white screams and biting teeth.

> Through the mists of memory
> You wander back to me

And when He arrived out of the purple mist He started to write it all down, He began to manipulate, to corrupt, purple still falling . . .

'I didn't do it,' Daniel had said, over and over again, trying to complete the column. 'It wasn't really me!'

And the memory had made him speak out loud again, the same hot and bewildered words, locked now in a car lost in the woods.

But, as before, the sound of his own voice released Daniel's limbs. He bobbed forward to switch on the windscreen wipers, without any conscious hope that their suddenly busy flick – fluck – flick would erase any part of his fear, any sticky blob of purple or any splattered segment of the things that the Author had made, is making or will make him do.

The wipers quickly cleared a patch and showed him that the path had suddenly widened, like a smile. The beech trees had been pulled back, no longer elephantine in their threat. Accusations thinned into the distance, where a faint glow of orange was pushing through the stalky horizon. He must have been most of the night on this track, driving round in a huge loop that repeated each detail of landscape, each patch of mind.

Daniel started to count numbers in his head.

And the headlights settled in a burning dazzle upon the low, shabby hump of an old building. An illumination.

The elusive cottage looked so old, so perfectly in place, so opportune in time and set that it might well have grown up out of the ground at the same time and the same rate as the surrounding trees. The presently denuded clumps of ancient beech and oak seemed now to be gesturing at one of their own, gnarled arms seeking to embrace the smaller dwelling. The trees were protective in their mood, gentle in their stance.

Daniel felt the tears rim his tired eyes. He had found what he had sought. He was not lost. There was, after all, a real place into which to retreat, a haven where he could do battle with or on behalf of himself. He had arrived. He had been allowed to arrive, rather. It was a permitted illumination.

*

The car stopped in a quiet slither, small wheels at first slipping on the new rain before they bit on the ridges of frozen mud underneath. His hands slackened. He sat still for a while, looking at the cottage and trying to smile. It was as though he wanted the building to acknowledge him. Those cold and worn stones, shining in the headlights, now represented every hope he had. They were the completed column. Some special quality of response was needed from that inanimate pile.

He waited, and he watched.

The noises of the woodland reached him now that the engine was silent. They were the sounds of rain on winter vegetation and, more familiar, on metal box and slate roof. Beyond or behind this drumming and hissing there were traces of less rhythmic patterns as aching timber adjusted to the wet and the cold and the first hint of distant light.

Daniel shivered, feeling the February cold at his marrow and a worse disappointment beginning to thicken in his veins. He was exhausted, and the cottage had already lost its first magic. Sheening in the lamps, glistening in the rain, it seemed to have become smaller and shabbier even as he had watched and waited. The remembered house, the awaited haven, was sending back no acknowledgement of his search, no subtle response as might a face or even a painting. It had already diminished into a sodden hump on the ground.

'It seems a very good idea,' Lucy had said. 'In theory.'

Oh, if only *she* was inside, expecting him, worrying about the delay, opening the door with a generous smile and warm arms. If only *she* understood. They would laugh and talk, touching each other. They would drink tea out of big white cups. They would . . .

'Get back!' she had hissed, eyes quick with fear.

'Bitch!' stepping towards her, ever and ever. 'Dirty fucking whore!'

'Daniel! No!' as her arm went up over her face.

He made a noise in his throat like a dog having a dream,

and then he snapped off the headlights. The cottage disappeared. Everything disappeared, sunk in the total darkness. The rain hissed and drummed in the overwhelming black.

'Lucy!' he called, before letting his teeth chatter with cold.

He felt with a thick hand at his cheek and found it as cold as a corpse, as when he had last touched his mother's flesh. The policeman had gripped his arm, just above the elbow, no doubt trying to communicate the statutory measure of sympathetic concern, briskly dispensed.

'Lucy,' he said again, in a quieter tone, unable to think of any other word let alone any other name, and confused as to whom he was really addressing, dead mother or separated wife, both out of his reach, both ignorant of the true nature of his love, both with arms protecting their gentle faces. How many times had he woken with the wrong name in his mouth? How many, many times had he stretched out alongside the wrong woman in the wrong bed?

It was so cold now, and still so dark, so bleak in spirit in this place, so empty between the bones of his being, that Daniel could at last feel that even the malignant Author had abandoned him to the incessant rain. Yet he experienced no release, no longed-for emancipation. If the Author had brought him here to do this to him then he knew that this was indeed the end, the real end. There would be no more pages. He was free, meaninglessly free.

He could count up to a hundred thousand million now, and beyond. There was nothing else which made sense. There was nothing else to do, nothing else at all. It was in any case too dark to examine the booklet of dirty pictures folded up in his inside pocket. They could not stir him now.

PART TWO

ACID AND LOLLIPOP

B̲ut. The word precedes every statement of feeling, every single expression of emotion. But, but, but . . . machine-gunning through our lives, my life.

My life?

I am surely correct in my assumption that I have after thirteen thousand and more words worked myself into a position where, for at least a few paragraphs or so, I can emerge from behind the misleading radiance of third-person omnipotence and begin to address you, the reader, more directly. But the important point to be grasped at once by all of you out there in the real world beyond these cold and shrinking walls is that I am not in any way *obliged* to make this shift: I choose to do so, openly and honestly.

These paragraphs, therefore, are in no sense a victory for the sick and guilt-ridden creature I had decided several months ago to call 'Daniel Miller'. He is stuck where I left him, and if I want to abandon him there, uncertainly oscillating between stripped woods and consulting room, then that will be his permanent state, his eternal dislocation. Too bad!

I will concede that characters in books do upon occasion

get out of control. They seem at these times to exist in some perverse dimension of metaphysics wholly outside or beyond the creative parameters originally laid down to contain all the possible variables of their being. But when this odd literary phenomenon happens it is usually because of the personal weakness or secret obsessions or (perhaps worst of all) blatant sentimentality of the author.

Miller has been and certainly will be denied such advantages as these. He remains an aggregation of words. I am, in short, totally in control of my material, properly or professionally unmoved by the temptations of that tasteless and soft-headed 'pity' which so often masquerades as 'compassion' (i.e. sentimentality) and completely stable in my personality.

Thus, Miller (as I will continue to call him) was in one sense correct in 'his' claim – designed to appear at first sight so ludicrous or even insane – that he was being written about, pinned down, by some vastly superior force or person. I *am* superior in the unarguable sovereignty of reality as I hold this pen, put in a comma, complete a sentence, dab down a full-stop: a person capable of controlling and manipulating all the other 'people' Miller has met, is meeting or will meet in this work. I can also shift or adjust the landscape itself (quite arbitrarily) within which he appears to live or (if I so wish it) to die. This helplessness, after all, is the ignominious lot of all fictional characters, for they are in plain logic doomed to be figments of the imagination. To claim any greater susbstance for them would be to invite a proper derision.

But (the machine-gun word), but I have taken careful note of an increasing Philistinism in the literary world which ignorantly or wantonly insists upon blurring beyond clear separation the necessary distinctions between the life and thought of an author and the words or feelings of his characters. These lice-like critics chomp out amateur psychiatry from their slavering, halitostic mouths for all the world as though they knew what they were talking about. And these ill-educated creatures have in the deft use of their jargon become so influential that even the ordinary, open-minded reader possessed of the normal modicum of plain decency is frequently misled into sharing the vulgar – indeed, preposterous – error of supposing that what one writes in fiction or drama is (how extraordinary!) what one *is*. As though words were as much a part of one's body as an eye or a leg or an arm or an even more private member!

At this present moment I am aware as never before in my life that I have to be especially vigilant in escaping the utterly inexplicable malice of most, if not all, of my former friends and acquaintances.

I have therefore intervened so early in my own narrative in order to stifle the dangerous kind of nonsense and critical confusion identified in the above paragraphs: the direct link, that is, between the real life of the writer and the invented life of his characters. The horrifying fact is that my erstwhile friends will seize only too eagerly upon certain segments of this book in order to demonstrate to the widest possible audience that the vicious things they have (to my certain knowledge) been saying about me are true. I can imagine the glee with which they will pounce upon this or that sentence, eyes bright with malice, mouths wet with cruelty. Let me emphasize again, therefore, with all the force it is possible to command, that only a fool or a charlatan will maintain that an author and his leading character are genetically or spiritually conjoined by things darker and stronger than the sweet grace of pure creative imagination.

Fools and charlatans abound, however. They have inherited the earth. And they will without doubt find scraps of information, shades of colouring, lapses of the tired hand or ambiguous asides within the preceding pages which they can inflate beyond all proportion to show to those who do not know me disgusting similarities between the wretched Miller and myself, his begetter.

I am, of course, well aware that good writers with any honest sensitivity or feeling for the complex structure of the processes of creation will certainly be among the first to acknowledge that their characters and their scenarios do indeed owe much of the incidental detail and some of the substance of the life within them to the personal experiences, anguish, hope, vision or actual memory of the author. But these writers, the good ones, would also go on to insist that such links are extremely loose or almost accidental: if they had wanted to write their autobiographies then they would have done so. Does anyone suppose that Dante really descended into Hell?

My own prejudice, for what it is worth, is that autobiography is with rare and famous exceptions the most brutishly inadequate of all the various literary forms, inherently dishonest (especially when being most conspicuously 'honest') and clearly spawned out of the unworthy desire to justify past error, past vice, or so to embellish previous guilt and humiliation with special pleading that it ends up between covers as something entirely different, something much more creditable to the writer.

Secret autobiographers, hiding behind the skirts of their invented characters, are even more contemptible. They lack even the crude audacity of their more overt colleagues. They pervert fiction by playing hide and seek with themselves and with their readers.

But the myth persists that most first novels are in large part autobiographical, and I again wish to make it absolutely clear beyond any reasonable argument that such a lazily modish observation cannot *in honesty* be made about this particular piece of literature.

Honesty is a virtue in short supply within the putrefying corpse of the poisoned octopus which slimily tentacles the London literary scene. I am convinced that it would be useful and prudent, therefore, if I now put down as directly and truthfully as possible at least a few of the more crucial similarities *and differences* between the character called Daniel Miller and the real person who is myself.

This task is tedious, but necessary. My lawyer will in due course be able to use this material in the libel or slander actions which I shall almost certainly be compelled to bring against some of my former acquaintances, and one of them in particular. (Far be it from me to clutter these pages with extraneous material or uncharitable interpolations, but I feel justified in indicating here that this particular person is the lank-haired lout with smelly feet and an irritating sniff, sniff who is responsible for forging the ridiculous love letters supposedly written by me to a syphilitic television actress and now circulating around London for the sniggery enjoyment of all those highly promiscuous parasites who pad their way along the rubbery corridors of the electronic entertainment whorehouses.)

Even so, I would not have bothered to make this list of similarities and differences if the first part of what had been intended as a literary experiment of some interest to others besides myself had not already been delivered to my agent after innumerable and seemingly very urgent requests 'to see at least something on paper', and if I had not through my own alert intelligence discovered on this very day that my agent – who was the one friend of long standing whom I thought in my foolishness that I could trust absolutely – is in fact a leading member of the envy-ridden and sex-obsessed faction which has somehow or other contrived to organize itself into a conspiracy that, alas, is attempting to oppress, degrade and humiliate me to the point where I will no longer be able to function as a talented and highly original writer, perhaps the most gifted of my generation.

The first and most obvious similarity which will be too avidly noted regarding Daniel Miller and myself is that we were both born and bred in the Forest of Dean. Putting it more accurately, *I* was born in that humpy green heart-shape of land between the two rivers. Miller was born only in my head.

Rather lazily, perhaps, I chose for self-evident reasons of convenience to make my imaginary character 'remember' a childhood spent in the same small region. In the circumstances this was a careless mistake on my part. But, then, think of all the research a writer such as Flaubert put into the treatments or characteristics of someone with a club foot! Every novelist with an ounce of integrity in his soul dearly wants and strives for the background of his story or the texture and 'feel' of his settings to be as authentic as possible. That is why we get so few English novels located in places like a Tibetan monastery, a Peruvian tin mine or the Ford Motor Works at Dagenham.

A flicker of caution which I dismissed at the time as entirely paranoid in its origins almost made me decide at the beginning of this project to put the cottage or the retreat high up and windswept in some lonely and uncontaminated valley (if such still exist) in the Lake District. I believe that I was right to rule against this in the end because I am only familiar with the region in a second-hand or guidebook or literary manner, principally through the works of Wordsworth (great man except when he called Coleridge an ABSOLUTE NUISANCE in impertinent capitals) and that snidely euphonious gossip De Quincey. My original conception was that Miller (though that was not then his name, incidentally) could journey to the Lakes ostensibly to escape the wen and its brothels by immersing himself in a new critical biography or *étude d'ensemble* of William Wordsworth. But it would have been even more crucial in that event to get the background seismographically accurate in all its mood, movement and topography unless one were to asphyxiate the sense of place with the so easily detectable smell of musty libraries and university lecture rooms. Any such absurdity would be an unpardonable offence against a landscape that surely still carries about its peaks and crags and abandoned sheep-folds the departed spirit of the poet.

No, the Forest of Dean made more sense as a location for my running man, my guilty cripple. Forests also have about them the power of ancient metaphors and inextricably tangled mystery, so similar to the human mind and yet so disturbingly alien to the normally gregarious human personality. We have an old instinct that calls upon us to worship the bountiful trees and also a contradictory and probably even older impulse to fear the forest dark and drear. A person does not choose the place where he was born any more than he can decide upon the colour of his eyes but I count myself fortunate to have first seen the light of day in that particular part of England, and it would have been a criminal waste to have allowed paranoid fears to force me into setting my book in any other place.

Those who make too much of the geographical link between Miller and myself are therefore, in a real and shameful sense, making too little of it as well. In concentrating so venomously upon the personal they forfeit all ability to recognize the universal or the elemental which belongs to any genuinely felt sense of place. But, then, these metropolitan charlatans are themselves so rootless and alienated (to use their own cant terminology) that they are incapable of chorographing any landscape which stretches beyond the confines of speckled pavement or painted bedroom. They will rest their heads on any available pillow as long as it is suitably perfumed and would probably use a vaginal deodorant on clinging ivy. Ignorant sods.

When the Lake District went silently out of my mind, Wordsworth receded too. Miller was then given the for him illusory ambition of completing a book about Coleridge instead. There is no great significance in this.

I will concede that, yes, there was once a time when I

44

seriously considered and even announced in a crowded room of admirers the idea that I would write a critical biography of Coleridge. It would be a base ingratitude on my part if for defensive reasons I now sought to deny this or to disown in any way the sustaining and emancipating pleasure or enlightenment which I have found in this writer. Indeed if I can ever get away from this place I do not rule out the possibility that I may yet return, refreshed and uplifted, to sing his praises and unravel his more prosaic obscurities. My agent – who by that time will suffer the chagrin and financial loss of being my *former* agent – knows this, because I recently mentioned it to him in a Fuller's tea shop. He will of course be among the first to point out with a nicotined finger that Miller, too, is supposedly engaged in writing up an *étude d'ensemble* of Coleridge.

> And all who heard should see him there,
> And all should cry, Beware! Beware!

The lines should have popped into my head as I watched him shovelling sugar into his tea. Some cream from one of the soft cakes stuck on his Mex moustache, but I was so engrossed in telling him of Coleridge at the most impetuous time of his twenty-third and twenty-fourth years in the West Country that I did not mention the blob of white stuff on his hairs. I wish now that I had wiped it off with one hearty smack across the mouth. I am glad that he paid the bill.

I could just as easily have made Miller write about Hazlitt or Southey or De Quincey, for I know a lot about all of that particular group. They lived and worked in more literate, letter-writing, road-walking days when relationships between writers could be at least as complex and fevered, as predatory or self-abasing or mutually illuminating, as any which more naturally exist between lovers appalled and delighted by the delicate equilibrium of their dependence upon each other. Writers nowadays talk to each other in idiot monosyllables on the telephone, or droop over melamine-topped tables in dream-factory canteens holding their heads in their hands. We have lost too much, and lost it forever.

What links can be made with my own soul by making Daniel Miller write about Coleridge or about Wordsworth or Hazlitt or Southey or De Quincey? None at all!

It would have been much easier still for me to fall back on the shoddy old device of arranging for my fictional character to be a writer of fiction himself: in truth, this mirror-like method (for all its previous misuses) lends itself excellently to some of the central concepts with which I originally embarked upon this present journey. But Miller is, to me, such a sick and weak creature, perpetually trying to blame others for his own foul behaviour and mental inadequacies, that I feared he would be left without any redeeming features whatsoever. I decided, therefore, to temper at least some of the bad which festers like running bed-sores inside him with at least one gift, one especial grace: Samuel Taylor Coleridge.

Thus, what is obviously meant to be a mature and harmonious gesture of creative benevolence, or a subtly transposed form of tribute to a great poet and critic, must not later be turned into a kettle of offal by untalented, uneducated and ill-disposed louts who would cheerfully fart in my face rather than acknowledge my skill or concede their own vile biliousness.

A few more points: that Daniel Miller and myself are almost exactly the same age is, to any reasonable mind, a trivial detail scarcely worthy of mention. I will not waste words in justifying an altogether unremarkable preference for choosing to write about a contemporary rather than inventing a character of an entirely different and therefore to some extent alien generation. If anyone should be stupid enough to dwell on this point he will succeed only in revealing for all to see the malice in his own mind.

Similarly, the fact that I too went to Oxford University is, in normal circumstances and in conditions of ordinary goodwill, a matter of only passing relevance. Very little is made of this humdrum similarity in the book, as you can check for yourself without difficulty. But intolerable and incredible though it is, this is just the sort of random or coincidental 'link' which will be held up as a further example of the allegedly self-exposing nature of my work!

Yet indignation, however righteous, is an enemy of clear thought and so of lucid expression, the two interpenetrating qualities which I value above all others. The lack of them is destroying our civilization.

I propose, therefore, to let the flame die on my cheeks. I will now gather up my walking stick, put on my gloves and go for a steady, calming walk as far as Hammersmith Bridge. It is extremely cold in this room, anyway, due to a misunderstanding with the bureaucrats who mismanage the electricity supply. A walk in the winter air will improve my circulation, clear my eyes, and allow me a little more time to think about the material which is now (thanks to my own trusting nature) in the hands of a man whom I would like to see floating face down in the dirty river.

One day, perhaps. One day. I am, after all, my father's son . . .

There ought to be a space or an empty page or maybe even a change of typography to show that I have been for the past three and a half hours out in the streets or sitting full of thought on that gilded and trembling bridge over the sleazy waters. At any other time I would probably telephone my agent and discuss this point for twenty minutes or so, for it is the kind of marginal detail which intrigues me and has never appeared to bore him. But I must readjust to the new and increasingly painful realization that this man is no longer to be trusted, not even in the smallest detail. Even a discussion about typography or paragraph spacing would be clouded with danger and twisted by subtle probings or innuendoes.

As it happens, the telephone does not appear to be working.

The 'untalented, uneducated and ill-disposed louts' I described above in rather intemperate language before taking my walk will make much of the 'coincidence' (as they will put it, with heavy irony, drawing out each syllable like bubble-gum) that Miller also appears to share the outward marks of my own alleged ill-health. This is a serious point, and I sat on the bridge thinking about how to settle it once and for all.

Readers with even rudimentary medical knowledge will be aware that swollen joints, clenching hands and itching or scaling skin are among the baleful symptoms of advanced psoriatic arthropophy. There is a misunderstanding abroad that I also suffer from this unpleasant ailment. This is not so.

In actual fact my walking stick and gloves are (I am almost too ashamed to admit) an elaborate affectation which has by degrees grown into such a habit that I find it difficult, if not impossible, to lay them aside. My father used to crack his finger knuckles like dry firewood, first as a joke, later as a tiny defence against boredom, and finally as a habit as much a part of him as his ear-lobes or the blue coal-scar tipped into the bridge of his nose. So it is with me, stuck with gloves and stick as soon as I step out of the front door.

A few remarks of mine in the past about the nature of my so-called 'disease' were simply rather embarrassed asides to explain away this foolish affectation. I am sure that with only a little effort of the imagination you can understand how these things can grow, can become set. We all have our little gestures, our tiny props. The undramatic origins of my particular badges, as it were, have been forgotten by everyone except myself. The plain truth is that I once twisted my knee after falling down a ridiculously narrow flight of stairs at a crowded party in a terraced house in Highgate, and I found it so comforting and indeed so peculiarly *elegant* to lean on a good stout walking stick during the weeks that followed this mishap that I continued to do so long after my leg had returned to normal. The gloves seemed to go with the stick, as any outfitter will readily confirm. I once went to the trouble of having a pair made in the finest white doeskin but fortunately I have now outgrown such extravagances in much the same way that I have outgrown the petty conversations and banal posturings of those who frequent literary gatherings or, worse, television studio canteens.

I visited this nasty ailment – the one I have not got – upon Daniel Miller in order to show how the guilt or evil in his mind finds physical expression in and on his body. If I had done the things he has done, if I had copulated with whores so indiscriminately and shamelessly, then I too would expect to find some signs of such evil upon my frame. But I am perfectly healthy, apart from a wisdom tooth which aches after I drink something too cold and an occasional headache if I work too long in a poor light. I am sorry to say I have such a headache at this very moment because the thin winter light has faded outside the window and I have had to light a candle in order to get all this down in good time.

The relationship between sin and sickness is uncompromisingly acknowledged in the book of common prayer, and it is a salutary one. I, for one, accept that dark bond as a true covenant between God and humanity.

'It wasn't me,' a man can say after some foul abomination such as hitting his wife or putting his penis in a prostitute's dribbling mouth, 'It wasn't really me. I am not responsible.'

So many say these things, as Daniel Miller says them. But what the flapping tongue denies the pain-scorched limbs confirm. The illness of Miller is directly attributable to his conduct. Not all of this man's behaviour has yet been revealed, of course, but I can assure you that there is one incident to come which in itself justifies almost any degree of the pain that has

49

so far been applied to his brain and his skin and his bones. He who touches pitch shall be indelibly stained with pitch, and dogs who return to their own vomit will be sick again and again. Come, lovely pestilence!

I could have infected Daniel Miller with any one of a host of fascinating ailments. It is ridiculous to be vindictive towards a fictional character but I must admit that contemplation of some of the available illnesses was a not altogether unpleasant preliminary to beginning this present work. There is a sombre euphony in the very names of sickness: think of hemato-lymphangioma and lienunculus and macrogenitosomia and phacocele, where pain hides in classical syllables, and throbbing nerves or ruptured tissues are given the dignity of the languages of antiquity.

Since I am perfectly fit myself I had to consider Miller's tribulation with some care, for I am here putting a foot on to an unknown terrain – always an exhilarating experience for a writer. I disdained to consult a medical dictionary, however. My friends yield up enough evidence of sickness. Indeed, it sometimes seems to me that the whole of this big, cold city is full of cripples, lunatics and the walking wounded. The polluted streets are crowded by people with pasty faces, running noses, rheumy eyes and strange, jerking motions. Whoever it is on the other side of this white wall, for instance, spends most of his waking hours wheezing and coughing and (by the sound of it) banging his swollen head against the partition.

I could have punished my whoremonger with some disgusting venereal complaint, but that would have been far too simple. In the present climate of opinion these old guardians of morality have in any case lost too much of their terror. Two weeks ago I wrote to the Archbishop of Canterbury suggesting that it was now time for the Church Militant to denounce antibiotics in the same uncompromising terms once used against usury, but I suspect my advice (admittedly unsolicited) will go the same way as the seed of Onan.

Miller had to have an illness which was visible, painful, incurable, distasteful to others and yet not even remotely acceptable as a 'status' ailment, such as duodenal ulcers, a disorder rather too fashionable among business executives, mass-communicators, literary agents and other money-grubbing vandals. I hope that by now you can begin to appreciate the delicacy of discrimination and the moral fervour which I have sought to bring to my work and that you will hold these qualities in your mind when the grossness, vulgarity and immorality of gossip or criticism begins to corrode the lucid purity of my text.

Visible, painful, incurable, distasteful to others – not such an easy task as one might think, for most of the internal ailments do not measure up to these basic requirements. I am leading you along the path I had to tread to find the most suitable disease, for only in this way can I be sure that the reader understands the nature of the ultimate decision and the ludicrousness of any attempt to confuse it with my own stick and gloves or any prior misinformation regarding the state of my own health. In this, especially, Miller and I have *nothing* in common.

I almost wish now that I had settled for chronic asthma with which to punish Miller, dispensing with the limp and the sausage fingers altogether.

Asthma has a great many things in its favour so far as my present purpose is concerned. I took at least two hours before reluctantly passing it over. This illness can be frightening in its sudden, panting melodrama, outward struggle of a diseased bronchial tree. I played around with these harsh gasps for a while, seeing Miller as a big pink fish stranded on a cobble-stoned beach, letting broken scraps of dialogue decorate the page. But, alas, the printed word cannot adequately convey the panting, gasping misery of this particular torment. And so although the disease fits my prescription, and although it too can be usefully linked with a skin complaint (eczema) which also flakes away at the body's surface, I had to abandon asthma. What cruel irony it will be if my own uncompromising and innovatory integrity should lead me into the mantraps set by the sort of people who scarcely know one end of a pen from another. It will not even pass through their minds that I spent so much trouble and thought on choosing the right disease or the most just punishment for my fictional character. All they will see is the walking stick.

Yet even migraine detained me with its potential, at first because of the popular assumption that it is above all a neurotic disorder and therefore confined to unstable personalities. Certainly, the illness would have given me plenty of opportunities to make strings of fireworks fizzle and explode in bright, whirling wheels of sulphurous pain in and behind Miller's word-jellied eyeballs. I understand, too, that the poor migrainee when under attack has tremendous difficulty in hearing and seeing the normal, outside world. Sound and light distort. Travel is impossible. The sense of balance is put at peril. My forest of trees could indeed have been turned into a forest of nerves, with each jagged branch poking into that guilty skull like the accusing fingers of God's darker or more vengeful angels.

Migraine, too, is followed by nausea and vomit rather as sin is followed by remorse. But can I really maintain that the affliction is 'visible, painful, incurable, distasteful to others' . . .? No. My choice had to be made with the greatest care and the most alert diagnostic skill. The troubles of the spirit are not always translated into the grosser medium of the flesh, but if I could not make this transfer with Miller then there would be no point in making him ill in the first place.

And why should he escape? Why shouldn't the dirty and degenerate suffer at least some of the consequences of their thoughtless self-indulgence and needless promiscuity?

All my research pointed in one direction: psoriatic arthropophy. I am assured by a rather unkempt doctor of my casual acquaintance that this disease – which neatly combines as in a two-thonged whip the miseries of arthritis and psoriasis – is a classic 'stress' illness, visible, painful, incurable and distasteful to others. It meets my fundamental requirements all along the line. I can without excessive licence properly regard the illness as sin made manifest in bone, guilt outcropping in itchy red layers on the skin, shame bubbling in hot pain in the ligaments. Stress which twists and deforms, which scrapes and creaks, burns and throbs.

I am going to light another candle now, for the first one is guttering in gold. I need more certain light in which to catch and express the sense of exultation which has suddenly come upon me.

The key word, of course, is *stress*. This is the force which I am applying so relentlessly to Daniel Miller, this is the power he is trying to escape on his bumpy journey into the winter woodlands. Understandably, he is looking for a place where he cannot be reached, A Retreat where he can enjoy an unearned or undeserved equilibrium. It would be weak sentimentality for me to allow him such grace.

You do not have to be tough minded or sombre in mood to acknowledge the truth that the whole concept of A Retreat, in the older senses of the phrase, is now redundant or used up, gone out of mind.

There are no more quiet corners left for us to discover. Where, now, can a man, even a good man, find peace? Not in a great cathedral nor in a doll's house, not in the tumult of a strange new city nor in the once sanctified words of a tough peasant stalking the sour hills of Judah. All contemporary hues, every scrap of modern dialogue, every present mood, every tabloid headline, every bell clanging across the meadow tells us this. We cannot take a chair out into the garden and expect to escape, not even with librium capsules as luminous as the lilac.

If panic dropped petals like a rose and if anxiety could flower in a forsythia bush then all the loveliest gardens in all the safest suburbs would bloom, bloom with every variety of stress. Everything I read, everything I hear, everything I see informs me that doubt, disease and distress in all the subtlest malignancies of their forms have at last invaded the cropped lawn and the sleepy garden wall. Stress it is which poisons the innocent spangles of daisies, dissonantly warps the song of the idiot birds or leers gibberingly over the useless privet. I can hear it like the constant traffic noise below my window.

Miller does not yet know this, the poor fool. He still thinks it possible to escape.

But if what I have said by the light of a new candle is true – and who can doubt it? – then even the elderly beeches and majestic old oaks of a remembered Forest of Dean are not capable of withstanding the fungoid of stress or the vegetable odours of spiritual decay. Guilt, cosmic guilt, stains the knobbly bark. Miller has already discovered it clinging like a woodpecker to the skin of the tree.

There is no just reason why he should escape. I would be failing in my duty if I allowed him such undeserved relief. And 'duty', heavily antique or even moth-eaten word though it has become, thanks to the mockery of charlatans, is the one proud constant which informs and dignifies both my work and my life. A virtue which, I realize, makes me too vulnerable, but I am not going to discard it now.

There is a gap again because I stopped work, suddenly aware that an alien indignation was invading my soul. I have no wish to get angry with my own invention, the so-named Miller. My contempt is aimed at other and *real* people, those who by their looks and whispers and complicated innuendoes have forced me to write what I had no desire to write. I do not yet know in what form this particular section will be published, whether as a foreword or as an interpolation into the body of my work, but I can begin to see that even here I can make something triumphant out of necessity. I have been reading the last few pages and I think they are true and beautiful and just, recompense enough for the cold gloom of this untidy and lonely room.

I have four cigarettes left and I need many more. Also I would give half the furniture in this room for a good strong cup of steaming hot coffee and a couple of aspirins. But the gas has been cut off, which is an appalling piece of vindictiveness on the part of some public servant who ought to know that writers of talent have better things to do with their time than remember dates on bits of paper delivered in brown envelopes like a trade circular. There ought to be a law against cutting off power supplies in the middle of February.

Still, I am working well. The words are coming out in the right order. More importantly, I can see that I am very effectively disposing of all the apparent or alleged similarities between Daniel Miller and myself. Age, health, background, education, interest in Coleridge – all this has now been put beyond possible confusion. I may also add, in passing, that Miller has brown eyes whereas I have blue, black hair where mine is red, good eyesight whereas I am a little shortsighted. He is also an inch or two taller than I am. Not even the most stupid policeman in the land could possibly mistake him for me in an identity parade, but I suppose I am being too optimistic in assuming that literary critics are likely to be more intelligent or perceptive than an ignorant cop. The columns of our newspapers and weekly journals are filled with book reviews or booksy gossip in which the hacks who write them seem determined before all else to carry on the one continuing tradition of their ignoble trade: ignorance.

I must not be too confident. I must explain a bit more, for other things occur to me as I try to recall the text which is now in the wrong hands.

Possibly, there are one or two apparent links between Miller and myself which I have not yet tackled, but most of these are mere trimmings, minor coincidences, or the accidental pen droppings, as it were, of an already admitted indolence so far as 'research' on unimportant detail is concerned.

It is this latter fault alone which explains the fact that rather than waste precious time in thinking up some other location I was lazily content to make Miller's London home a flat rather like the one in which I am now diligently at work, here in cruelly named Shepherd's Bush.

I do not need anyone to rub in the truth that, yes, I too dwell heavily suspended above traffic snarl, pavement noises, an eel-and-pie shop, a tobacconist's and a hardware store. But in the text of the novel Miller is described as living above all these premises *and an automatic laundry*. This is not the case with me. *There is no laundry on the ground floor*.

Is that not a crushing answer to those who would maintain that Miller and myself live in the same flat? Does this not silence them?

Furthermore, it is utter nonsense in any event to turn the mere similarity of habitation into a similarity of personality, for that would be to argue the proposition that if two people occupy the same room they thereby become exactly like each other in their minds and in their actions. Anyone who maintained such a preposterous theory would be considered mad, and rightly so!

The force of this logic outweighs even the absence of the automatic laundry, yet I have no alternative but to duplicate arguments or double-bank my defences. I keep brooding about this morning's telephone call to my agent. And although I am now tired, very cold and extremely hungry – with a headache into the bargain! – I am compelled to continue for a little while longer. Without coffee, without aspirin.

I suspect that the reader is by now getting confused or even angry. You have in your hands a book which starts clearly enough with a character trying to escape from his author and which has now reached the opposite pole with the real author (myself) trying to escape from his own character. But I hope you are amiable and fair-minded enough to accept that this switch was not in any way part of my original purpose. I have been dragged into my own book against my will. Without heating, without proper light.

There is without a shadow of doubt some very nasty gossip about me now sludging its filthy way through the intestines of the society I know and have come to despise. If I had not intervened on these pages to explain a few points this book (or its opening section) would be a gun aimed at my own temple. I do not see why I should so deliver myself up to those who are so assiduously conducting the campaign of abuse and denigration directed at me. You can surely sympathize with this self-protective caution, even if by the nature of the case you cannot wholly share it.

Indeed, you may even have heard some of these dirty rumours yourself. I hope not. But it now seems that people completely unknown to me, absolute strangers, have been giving me what my mother used to call 'old-fashioned looks' or furtive, sidelong glances.

I became vividly aware of this disturbing phenomenon while I was sitting deep in thought on Hammersmith Bridge this afternoon. A big, flat coal barge was passing under the bridge and I averted my eyes from the sight of it. As I did so I became aware of a youngish man with long hair looking at me from the pavemented walk on the Hammersmith side of the river. He was walking with a girl, a dark haired one with a red coat and white boots. He bent towards her, saying something, and then they both examined me intently before laughing to themselves and passing on.

The gulls were wheeling and crying above the parapets of the ornate bridge and for one mad moment I thought that they, too, were engaged in an elaborate mockery. I sat as still as cold wax, watching the grey river slug by towards the girdered floodlights of Fulham football ground. It was a bad moment and I had to put down a swift impulse to rush to the side and throw myself over.

Consider: the electricity has been cut off, the gas supply has stopped, the telephone has no dialling tone. I have not had a letter for at least a fortnight, whereas I used to get one or two every other day or so. Strangers bend their heads together to talk about me. If I stand at the window (which I am not going to do) I can see a small fat man with a trilby hat, a British warm and what looks like a binocular case, standing down below on the other side of the road and peering up with an anxious concentration at this battered, paint-peeling semi-circle of so-called Mansion Flats.

Consider these things, as I have. Ask the right questions.

I do not wish in a paranoid fashion to make too much of any one of these facts taken in isolation. But it is the most distinctive characteristic of an observant or well educated mind to bring unity to what would otherwise be a meaningless scatter of seemingly random and unrelated phenomena, and I bow to few for want of intellect. When the facts or events I mentioned above are put together in sequence, and when they are set into the background of recent developments, then a different and far more worrying interpretation begins to appear.

Everything which is now taking place confirms that I have to be careful, very careful, even to the extent of disowning some of my earlier work if necessary.

There are only two cigarettes left now. They have white filters, and I am concerned lest in this poor light I should mistakenly set fire to the wrong end. It would be a waste, and it would not taste very nice either. But I must not get irritable, must not. Things in themselves have no malevolence: only people. Let me tell you to what degree.

*

This morning I telephoned my agent from the kiosk on the corner of the road to make sure that he had received the first fourteen or fifteen thousand words of my novel and, hopefully, to hear him say that, yes, he thought a publisher would give me a worthwhile advance (much needed) on the strength or promise of this sizeable chunk.

By the time I had replaced the telephone in its cradle I had realized in a sudden, terrifying swoop of misery that I was in genuine danger. My agent had exposed himself as one of the conspirators. And there, on his desk, was a hostage of my self-respect, my social reputation, and even my sanity. I had walked straight into a hideous trap.

In case you think I am exaggerating I will try to put down on the page the conversation we held this morning, he in his warm office with his eighteenth century paperweight and leggy slut of a secretary and I in a dirty glass-doored box that might have been entered in an exhibition of unusual refrigerators.

'Did you get it?' I asked straight out, without greeting or preliminaries. I do not like using the telephone at the best of times and was never very fond of small-talk, that tedious lubricant for rusty little minds.

There was a tiny but – in retrospect – significant pause before he replied.

'Why ever didn't you bring it in yourself?' he said. 'We would have liked to see you.'

'Because I didn't feel like chatting,' I said in an amiable tone, 'I didn't feel like seeing anyone. Not until I got a reaction. This work is very important to me.'

'I see,' he said, drawing out the double ee. Then, swiftly, 'Listen – are you all right?'

'What do you mean?' I asked, getting that first warning flicker that something was wrong or out of place.

He laughed in that slow way of his, and it sounded to me as though he was turning his head away from the mouthpiece.

Probably to wink at the office slut, crossing her swishing legs.

'I mean are you *all right*,' he said, 'are you O.K.? Are you functioning?'

I gripped the telephone tightly and looked at my face in the little oblong mirror of the kiosk and could not, for a moment, think of a single thing to say. I had not looked in a mirror for a long time, not closely.

'I tried to telephone you this morning——' he said.

'Phone's not working,' I gabbled. 'Look – have you got it? Have you had time to read it? Is it any good?'

'It's good,' he said.

Never before had I heard him, or anyone else for that matter, sound so emphatic in praise of my written work. I had a peculiar feeling: it seemed as though a great golden salmon leapt up inside me, full of life and courage. It was a moment of such pure joy that I probably went pink with pleasure. I must have missed the next few sentences.

'——and weirdly compelling,' he finished, almost smacking his lips under that ridiculously trendy moustache.

'Do you think the publishers will give me an advance on it?' I plunged in. I could already see the books piled high in the better shops, garlanded with white slips of praise.

'I'm damned sure they will,' he said.

Usually he called my work 'promising' or 'almost too original' or 'full of potential' or 'a bit ahead of the market' or any one of those predictable, embarrassed and therefore embarrassing phrases which are meant to soften the fact that he thought he would not be able to place it anywhere 'for the moment'. It is, of course, the fate of all the truly talented to collect rejection slips from Philistines and cretins. But this time his confidence seemed so genuine, so unevasive, that I must admit I felt my throat tighten.

'I've been working very hard on it,' was all I managed to say.

'So that's what you've been hiding away for!'

'Hiding?' I caught at the word, as I was right to do. 'What do you mean – *hiding*?'

That slow laugh came again, but this time I could identify for sure the menace and the mockery in it. I tensed my body in the kiosk. The salmon had already turned into a ravening wolf, eating at my innards. How soon joy can turn into fear!

'Nobody has seen hide nor hair of you for at least a month,' he was saying. 'We all thought you were ill again. Or shacked up with a new girl you wanted to keep to yourself or something.' (Note, please, the 'we'.)

A fire engine went by the kiosk with that excruciating ooh-ah ooh-ah ooh-ah of urban alarm.

'Fire engine,' I said down the line, the harsh echo of the warning noise now reverberating in my brain.

'Pardon?'

'Nothing,' I mumbled. 'A fire engine just went by. I couldn't hear you properly.'

'Seriously, though,' he went on, perhaps put on his guard by the inadvertent change of tone in my own voice. 'I think it is a very bold and very clever piece of work indeed. I'm fascinated by it. You've never done anything better.'

I waited, my breath hanging in the cold, stale air of the telephone kiosk. I have found that if you keep still, if you keep quiet, then the other person feels he has to continue talking. You can uncover many things in this way, so long as you can hold your nerve when the technique is put into reverse and used against yourself. If the person I am with does not talk, then I do not talk.

'I rather like the way you are coping with that boring old hang-up of who or what the narrator of a novel is supposed to be,' he began again. 'You've tackled it head on by letting the main character *know* that he is being written about. I like that.'

'Yes,' I said. 'I'm sick to my stomach of novels, really. They are so fraudulent. They pretend to tell you too much. As far

61

as I am concerned novelists are almost as redundant as psychiatrists because both species have the same irredeemable impertinence. They are both disreputable practitioners of empty trades and I wanted to——'

'Yes,' he interrupted me. 'I get all that. I think.'

'Do you?' I asked, imprudently letting the smile of contempt tint my voice.

My agent is not the brightest of creatures, though like many middlemen in most trades he is usually able to hide this big hole in his mind with his trendy patter and strategic placing of the latest fashionable phrase or concept. He possesses what I call an 'art school mind', which is well on the soggy side of the truly intellectual. Quote a Latin tag at him by mistake and he will examine his shoes or smile brazenly back at you. I rarely find much satisfaction in debating harder abstractions or metaphysical teasers with him. In the last resort, of course, he cares only about his ten per cent and he would, I'm sure, much rather have Patience Strong than Christopher Logue on his books. But it is foolish to look for great intellectual nourishment from a parasite, just as it would be to expect the delicacies of romantic love in the company of a hired prostitute.

'Yes,' he said again, floundering in his own shallows. 'I can't wait to read the next chunk. I've got a feeling that the Author is waiting all the time in that house in the woods for His own character to turn up.'

'Cottage.' I corrected him, probably between my teeth.

'House, cottage – doesn't matter, does it? Cottage, yes. I hope the Author is already in residence, so to speak. Waiting to – well, God knows how you take it on from where you left it. Have you got it all worked out? The plot, I mean?'

I sniggered derisively. Plot? My God, these art-school minds betray themselves at crucial moments. Plot! Good God Almighty.

'What do you mean by that exactly?' I asked him, trying very hard not to laugh.

'You know what I mean.' He sounded quite testy. 'I don't mean every fucking twist and turn of the story line, now do I? I mean have you got a clear idea of the relationship between the so-called Author and his character. I take it I am correct in using the word "character" in both senses of the term?'

'Pardon?' I said, my neck starting to tingle.

'Well, I presume the character is also the Author's character. There's a – well, if I may be pompous, a sort of biochemical relationship between the two.'

'Biochemical?' My own voice this, helpless.

'If this Miller as you call him takes the tablets you keep on about in the text he will discover that there is no Author – right? He will know then that the Author is in fact himself, and always was. Right?'

I shouted that he did not know what he was talking about and held the telephone away from my face. At the same time I could hear someone tapping frantically on the glass door of the kiosk, someone far too anxious to clamber in with me. I felt what I can now see to be an unreasonable surge of panic. It was of course simple mischance that this rat-tat should happen, even though the kiosk is not so far as I know a particularly busy one.

'Hello! Hello!' I could hear that odious voice crackling. 'Hello? Hello? Are you there? Are you there?'

The bastard knew by now that he had given the game away. He was bellowing down the line like a demented station announcer.

If I had been sensible I should have hung up there and then. But a desire to be fair, a wish to be absolutely certain, and an understandable reluctance to accuse someone of perfidy who has been a friend of mine for six difficult years made me pull the telephone back to my mouth. I did it so vigorously, however, that I slightly cut my lower lip on the edge of the hard black instrument.

'Bad line, old mate,' I said, tasting my own blood.

The backs of my legs were trembling at that time, but this was probably as much due to the cold as to the feeling of betrayal that had invaded my being. I have not been really warm for days. This is the harshest February for many a long year.

'Look, why don't you hop on the tube and come on in and have a drink.' The voice was far too hearty. He must think I am a fool. I do not have a straw that is long enough to take a drink with *him*.

'You think Miller and I are linked in some way? Is that it?' I asked him.

'I said Miller and The Author, capital T, capital A,' he replied, still as smooth as syrup. 'But I think you have used some of your own pain very – um – well, with great skill and honesty. It creates quite another dimension – yes? Are you there?'

'I'm here,' I said, toneless. And someone was still tapping on the door.

'You've got all that additional tension which readers are bound to recognize,' he went burbling on. 'The way you weave in your own background, your own – um – illness, and that trouble or guilt Robert was trying to tell me about. I think it's a marvellous piece of work, honestly I do. You are facing up to yourself in a very moving and powerful way – hello? Look – come on in. We've all been a bit worried about you and I would love to see you. Hello? Hello?'

I waited a moment, letting him think the line was dead.

'You shitbag,' I then said, in a completely calm and level tone. I put the phone into its cradle, extremely gently.

I looked into the little mirror for just a moment. I had not realized until then that there were tears in my eyes. For a fraction of a second I felt that life itself was no longer endurable. I wanted to stay in that cold glass box for ever.

But I am also a resilient soul. Self-pity is a totally contemptible vice and I have throughout many vicissitudes and much unmerited disappointment avoided it as a plague. So I soon turned away, regretting only the loss of the shiny new tenpenny piece which I had inserted into the coin box to avoid any irritating *boop-boop-boop* cutting in to what I had stupidly hoped would be an uplifting and wholly encouraging conversation about my work and prospects.

'About bleed'n' time an' all.' snarled this sharp-faced old fellow as I stepped out of the kiosk.

Suddenly amused, I held the stiff door open for him and bowed languidly from the waist with an exquisite fin-de-siècle sarcasm, a little flourish of an unquenched spirit. Needless to say the gesture was neither understood nor accepted. The old man did look a bit shamefaced, however, but it was a worthless little triumph.

(You will have noticed, I trust, that there is no mention of my walking stick and my gloves in this kiosk episode, thus proving that I certainly do not *need* to use them. They are stage props, only.)

I walked slowly back up the shabby road to this now miserable room, thinking all the while of what I ought to do or what I *could* do if I was ever going to outmanoeuvre these cunning poisoners. You can appreciate by the remarks my agent made to me on the telephone (words which I swear I have not amended or distorted in any way at all) just how big and unpleasant a problem I have sitting like a gibbering troll on my innocent shoulders.

The winter wind skeetered viciously along the dirty pavement and the grey air was so thick with cold that it felt like frosted glass against the raw flesh of my face. But all the time my mind was working. During that painful walk I managed to work out the general outline of these pages. Yet even the most productive thoughts and even the bravest of responses to the new dimensions of my predicament could not wholly keep the chill out of my bones or push away the icier gloom from above my head. It was a bad moment.

> And through the drifts the snowy clifts
> Did send a dismal sheen:
> Nor shapes of men nor beasts we ken –
> The ice was all between.

Words from the past, images from the great, are better by far than any biochemical. I mounted the wide stone stairs of this block with Coleridge back in my mind.

My one real consolation in the face of almost any betrayal or grief is that I am without doubt an extremely talented writer, come danger or candle stump. I always feel happier or calmer with a pen in my hand, for writing is the one activity which gives me an unquestionable dignity and, if I may dare to claim it, an unconquerable pride.

I do not at this precise moment, therefore, feel quite as wretched as I did this morning after using the public telephone or as bewildered and terrorized as I did this afternoon while sitting half-frozen on the trembling suspension bridge across the sleazy Thames. Mind you, I could do with a fire, an electric light, a packet of cigarettes and a good pot of coffee. But for all that the words are still coming out from under my fist, upward strokes and downward strokes proliferating like twig insects on the sheets of foolscap paper. So long as I keep it up I am still in charge of my own destiny.

The flame of the candle on this table is by no means an unpleasant light. The shadow of my hand quivers on the page. And within or without these dancing shapes and from deep within the brighter flame of my own imagination I can escape any pressure from any source. I can with a few deft strokes build myself a crenellated castle with coloured windows, or a maze of evergreen, or a field of rippling corn, or a fat blackbird with bright eyes picking at a cluster of red berries. I can do what I like on these pages, and nobody on earth can prevent me. Hallelujah!

I will not let in any person from Porlock. Not now. Not ever.

Exultation comes and goes, but here again for the while I suppose it has returned to me in preparation for that step back into the radiant arc of omnipotence which is only given on this earth to the narrator in or of a novel.

The sensation is a thrilling one, and I enjoy it immensely. I will be profoundly relieved when I can escape from the prosaic explanations and defences of this present sprawling mess of words. I am anxious to get back to the Forest of my own creation, my own memory, my own past and future hope.

Unlike Daniel Miller I do not have to go there in person. I am able to return to that blessed hump between the Severn and the Wye in ways which, in logic, Miller is prevented from enjoying. Not for him the pleasures or the relief of omnipotence! Not for him the emancipation and the exultation and the divinity of creative work!

Even if I allow him to scribble down a few paragraphs of his own fiction (and I do not see why I should) it still follows that any words he might write must in the first instance be composed by me. He is trapped as I cannot be trapped. There is no way in which he can free himself from my control, not unless I lose my nerve or allow him to be abducted by some plagiarist, and not unless I allow any of my own present personal dilemmas connected with my own personal escape to lodge unbeknown to me in the words which make up this fictional character.

For this latter reason alone it is crucially important as a matter of artistic integrity that Miller, the invented man, does not have too much in common with me. He must only be alive between the covers of a book, and not anywhere else.

I am reasonably sure that by this time any fair-minded reader with a spark of decency will readily acknowledge that all the *apparent* similarities between Daniel Miller and myself have been more than satisfactorily explained. It is now possible, therefore, for us to come to the all important *differences* between my character and myself. There are quite a few people in this town (my agent included) who will feel pretty sick or even shamefaced (I hope!) when presented with this coming segment. Spiteful gossips, scandalmongers, churls and hypocrites – please read on, if you dare.

Considerable and conclusive differences in height, in health, in hair and eye colouring have already been noted in the text. Miller, in short, does not even *look* like me. We would not even pass for distant cousins let alone members of the same nuclear family unit. He is not my brother but I *am* his keeper.

'You've got all that additional tension which readers are bound to recognize,' burbled that smug art-school voice on the telephone this morning. 'The way you weave in your own background, your own illness, and that *trouble or guilt* Robert was trying to tell me about . . . you are *facing up to yourself* in a very moving and powerful way . . .'

There you have it! I have no doubt that masked remarks and hints such as these will be tinder for all the combustible muck which has already been piled high around my reputation. The attack, in other words, is far more subtle than just pointing out any supposed physical resemblance between Miller and myself. These people know that I can dispose of all that. What they will say, and probably are already saying, is that no matter what else may be dissimilar there is in fact a shared experience, a shared guilt, a similar anguish or torment, an identity of sin and shame and former behaviour between Miller and myself.

'That trouble or guilt Robert was trying to tell me about . . .': here, almost fully out in the open now, brazenly direct, we come to the gangrenous core of the rotten, shit-smeared campaign directed at me.

I can hardly bear to write this down. I feel almost too sick to continue. The odour of that gossip, the stench of that incomprehensible malice, seems to fill the room. Nausea swirls up at my nostrils. Disgust invades me, invades this room, almost like a real reptile, a skink flicking out its swift purple tongue. There is something slithering along these shadowed walls and I can remember against my will the shock and the smell of seeing the steaming intestines pulled from a slaughtered pig, a poor animal with skin like a human being.

I managed to get down the last two words of the preceding paragraph before my stomach over-boiled into my mouth. I rushed down the dark passage to the lavatory with both hands at my face. I do not ever recall being quite as sick and shaken as I was then, about an hour and a half ago. It was as though the very innermost lining of my already emptied stomach was violently detaching itself into long, coppery green strands of rejected bile. I was as helpless and as degraded as the pig on the bench at the top of our garden nearly thirty years ago.

I, too, began to fear for my life as I stooped over the lavatory bowl. I felt that I was being turned inside out. It did not seem that I could survive such a volcanic attack from deep within my own system. But who is there to care about that? Who would be capable of writing my obituary without malice? Who is that being here in London who could throw the cold earth on my coffin without a smile on his or her face? Who would even remember my name twelve months from now in the midst of another winter, unless in the context of some old dirty joke or dated ribaldry?

The brutality of these questions and, at what was virtually the same moment, the icy coldness of the tapwater on my face restored me, gasping, to a renewed sense of the value and purpose of my own existence.

I know now that I have a duty to look after myself, for no one else will bother. I can see that I will have to get away from this stinking city with its endless acres of asphalted rumour, its

tenements of whores and pimps, its traffic in misery and its
festering suburbs of ding-dong doorbelled malice. Surely
there are cleaner places inhabited by more wholesome people
somewhere on this island? I am not asking for Camelot, after
all. I do not expect King Arthur to rise fully accoutred from
the cave in which he lies asleep, any more than I expect my
father to clamber out of his shallow pit of prison lime.

All the time I was convulsed by sickness in the dark lavatory
someone kept knocking and hammering and ultimately even
kicking on the front door of this flat. I know who it must have
been.

I do not propose to open my own door to any such snoop-
ing interlopers, disturbers of my peace. I could not have
opened it then in any case, for that would have been a physical
impossibility – tempting though the picture is of the evil
creature on the other side of the door getting a well-deserved
spasm of slimy stomach bile heaved right up into his florid
and trendily moustachioed face. That's one ten-per-cent he
can have with pleasure!

'That trouble or guilt Robert was trying to tell me about . . .'

Dear God, it is astonishingly cold in this room. My fingers
are as white, alabaster white, as the hands of a corpse. If I
speak out loud my breath hangs in the candle-light, just as
though one could snap off a word in a mistily solidified lump
as soon as it has been said. Would that we could as easily
gather back all the things we have said in mistake over the
years, gather them in and powder them down until not one
trace of their original form is left.

I am going to put my hands above the slenderly tapering
flame of the candle for a moment. It is the only source of
warmth in the room.

*

I think now of the way the shaggy but emaciated-looking, dull-eyed sheep who wander so wearily about the paths and tracks of the Forest of Dean find their way into the brick bus shelters on nights such as this. They huddle sensibly together in heaps of dirty wool while the pitiless wind shifts and howls between the shivering trees or flaps with daemonic aggression at the corrugated sheets of the sheds, outhouses and garages along the village road. I could do with their company at this moment. I want to share in that ordinary, uncomplicated animal warmth, free of human complexities or human odours, their breath sweetened with the juices of twice-digested grass and other comely vegetation plucked from remembered waysides.

But the one thing I will certainly not find in Shepherd's Bush is a real, live sheep! So much for names, so much for words. They so often have long since lost the literal meaning of their origins, and thus they are frequently capable of causing gross confusion and comic misunderstanding.

The manner in which one says or writes things, those public and therefore never totally adequate ways in which we seek to express our private or inner emotions, always has an implicit as well as an explicit content. You know as well as I do that we can too easily by intonation or facial expression or (the prose equivalent of those signals) by the precise positioning of a single word in the surrounding thicket of language make the simple statement 'I love you' mean 'I own you, despise you, exploit, deceive or hate you' just as the equally plain 'I hate you' can be picked up as 'I fear, envy, respect, despise, own, exploit, deceive or love you, love, love you.' This inherent ambiguity of all language lies coiled at the root of my present troubles.

Four or five months ago on a gentle Autumn evening I climbed some steep stairs in a converted house in Holland Park to call upon my then closest friend and ally, the Robert whom my agent mentioned so cunningly and cruelly in his self-exposing telephone conversation this morning. We were at Oxford together, Robert and I, and have often talked the night away in former times, mingling literature and politics and cheap red wine with the cigarette smoke and the laughter and the brittle pile of old Al Bowlly records he had stumbled upon in a junk-shop kept by a one-time Polish airman. Oh, how love and trust can be betrayed! How friendship can be corrupted!

It was there, while the starlings chattered outside his tall windows, there in Robert's amiable clutter of a room, that I *appeared* to confess to him some unpalatable and, indeed, extremely degrading 'facts' about myself.

I will go so far as to concede that taken in isolation, ripped away from the defining context of humour and irony and friendship, studied in their literal or surface sense only, then, yes, the words I spoke in that room as Robert stood at the window pretending to take me seriously *could* be understood to mean that during the past six or seven years I had gone to bed with more than one hundred and fifty prostitutes. I may even have said in the spirit of the joke that it had been one hundred and fifty-six whores, for all the world as though it was of an obsessive importance for the actual number to be known with absolute accuracy! This is the way one over-embroiders invention when playing complicated verbal games or intellectual hide and seek with one's closest friends. Robert, especially, knows this, for he knows the style of my speech as well as he knows the rhythm of my walk or the vocabulary of my gestures. He could not possibly have misunderstood me.

I realize that I need to work my way through the next passages with care and delicacy. Everything is *hinged* at this point. I have a duty to myself and to my reader to express what follows with truth and dignity. I must as a matter of honour remove all possible ambiguities of expression, avoid any taint of pretence, or dishonesty, or literary sleight of hand. The light may be flickering wildly, but my head must be clear, my thoughts steady. Now, as never before, I need to concentrate all my will and energy, all my talent and intellect, upon words on a page more important even than some petition for clemency composed under the shadow of the gallows.

But it is so vindictively cold in this ill-lit room, and my alabaster hand aches so much from the thousands of words I have put down on this unhappy day, and my head still throbs, and my stomach is so empty, and my grief is so heavy, that I think it would be wise of me to break off at this point, this hinge, blow out the once again guttering candle and for the third time today go down the stone stairs to streets where it is always February.

Very late though it is, there is a formica-clad coffee or hamburger bar still open less than half a mile away and I have enough cash in hand to buy my first food of the day and my first hot drink. I can sit in the warm and sip their hot froth of a brew for maybe the best part of an hour with any luck. Certainly, it will help me to think more clearly. I want to get the now constantly recurring image or memory of the scraggy sheep huddled together at night in the bus shelter off the top of my mind: it is disconcerting to be writing about one thing and yet be presented while doing so with quite another set of pictures. Coffee will help – blessedly hot liquid to scald or drown those shaggy beasts in the brick shelter so many miles away from here in the place I once called Home.

I sat in the coffee bar for a long time. Indeed, I sat there in the muggy warmth until the balding, bull-necked scruff of a proprietor or manager started to put the chairs upside down on the swabbed tables – a peculiar custom which is surely unhygienic enough to be banned by law. He yawned as he did it, and banged about a bit, so I felt that I had to go. But I had re-freshed myself.

The coffee, of course, was awful and the cheese sandwich I had enough to buy was probably made out of some new plastic rather than the milk churn. We are becoming a degenerate race, even in the simplest things. Our daily bread is concocted by chemists who do not sleep easy at night.

But the room was warm, brightly lit and by no means un-comfortable so long as you kept your eyes away from the map-like stains on the rancid blue walls or the cigarette ends and other scraps on the floor. The proprietor reminded me of the man who used to travel round the Forest villages killing pigs. He gave me a few quick, curious glances from time to time as I slowly sipped my coffee, but he did not appear to have heard any of the rumours. At least, I did not catch him whispering to any of the other people going in and out of the place, and he did not point me out to anyone at any time.

So as I sipped the barely brown dishwater he passed off as coffee (at a wholly extortionate price) I was able to thaw my limbs, re-line my stomach, rest my hand and ponder at length the best or most honest method by which to tackle the re-mainder of this difficult and embarrassing work of explanation.

For twenty minutes and more I could not think of a thing to write. I could scarcely think at all. I felt my eyelids begin to droop and the warmth of the room slowly turning into a soft buzz in my head, the sort of sound which so often precedes the sudden slip into sleep itself. It is possible that I even dozed off for a few seconds, exhausted by the day's work.

Instinct alone brought me back to alertness, a warning pulse from the innermost guardian of my being. As though the voice was directly in my ear again I surfaced out of the mo-mentary haze to hear my agent saying 'that trouble or guilt Robert was trying to tell me about'. I almost turned round, so clear was the tone, so near.

I dare not relax, not then and not now. There is still too

much explaining to do, no matter how cold and weary I may be feeling. This is the time for vigilance. As the buzz or the haze receded, and as I chewed the last tasteless fragment of sandwiched thermoplastic, I steadied myself by counting the melamine tables and counting the chairs and counting the customers and counting the sticky sauce bottles and the dome-shaped salt cellars and the cups, the plates, the cutlery, the ash-trays, anything in sight. The steady rhythm of numbers is im-mensely calming. Used properly the method empties the mind of everything extraneous. Out of such a sequence I began to put my thoughts into similar order.

My task, as I now see it, is to communicate the true nature of my attitude or (more important) my actual behaviour to-wards women. Only by this means can the rumours be judged according to their worth.

You do not know me and so you cannot be expected to take anything on trust. If Robert came to you and said in his gentle, somehow caressingly placid voice that I had admitted or con-fessed to him in 'obvious distress' that I had pushed my penis up between the hired legs of more than one hundred and fifty tarts (including three on one single day, or two on one single bed) then you would probably believe him. Prurience is uni-versal.

Furthermore, Robert has worked up the story very well. I would wager that he goes so far as to say that I broke down in his room, stuttering out the words of my so-called confession between chokes and tears, unable to speak properly. He puts himself in good light by adding that he gripped me tightly round the shoulders in reassurance, that he gave me brandy, that we talked long after the starlings had ceased their chatter, that we walked down into the street and discussed in jogging stride what guilt or shame or desire could do to the human soul.

It no doubt has an authentic ring, the way he tells it.

Doubly authentic, because I have often observed that where

these delicate questions are concerned most listeners are more inclined than not to accept the most improbable of two or three possible explanations for the vagaries of a person's conduct. People, to be blunt, have minds like sewers.

This unpalatable but, alas, essentially valid simile means that once an especially vile rumour has been launched there is all too little the wretched victim can do about it. The chances are that if you are told a nasty tale about the sexual misdemeanours of a headmaster, a vicar, a scout leader, a member of Parliament, a public performer or a novelist then you will assume it to be the truth. The Sunday newspaper hacks earn their livings on such gullibilities.

Robert would make a superb gossip writer. He always stands strategically in corners at parties or similar wasteful gatherings of the wasted, his glass tilted in his hand, his broad back against the wall, talking all the while in those low, resonant yet rather monotonous tones which everyone listens to with a sniggery sort of attention. He has the knack of purveying filth while appearing utterly detached or even incredulous about the content. I can hear him now, sniffing and purring under his lank hair, pretending to be full of 'compassion' or concern as he recounts the endlessly embellished details of my so-called iniquity. He will pause every now and then, rolling his large head a little, fingering the rim of his glass, tut-tutting deep in his throat, determined to convey the impression of a charitable fellow who is anxious to put the most favourable interpretation on the strange behaviour of his friends!

I was counting the chairs and thinking in distress about this odious scandalmonger, this heartless traitor, when I noticed the face of a young woman on the opposite side of the blue-walled coffee bar. She was sitting at a littered table with two noisy West Indians in colourful pullovers and a jaded, almost middle-aged fat lady with a fur coat. The girl's eyes did not at first stray in my direction so I was able in safety to look at her, to examine her, for quite some time.

I must have studied her with attention for I find that I can at this moment, however reluctantly, see her face before me as distinctly as though I was still sitting in that coffee bar with a quarter of an inch of the brown dregs left in my cup.

Why do faces loom up in this way? How is it that eyes or mouths or the most fleeting expression, the merest muscular twitch, rise unbidden to an otherwise fully occupied mind?

Sheep in a shelter, a pig on a bench, a woman on the well-stones, two men swinging their legs: why are they so persistent, why are they linked together? These must be what are called hypnogogic images, the strangely potent montages which come at a mind already lapsed into a sort of sleep.

I cannot yet rest. I cannot. I dare not.

Only by writing like this will I keep alert. The only times I do not want to be a writer are when I want to be a painter, and the only times I want to be a painter are when I am taken by the cast or mobility on a person's face. Usually a woman's face, like the face of the girl in the coffee bar an hour or two ago.

Her face is coming back to me yet again, reforming out of bouncing shadow.

But an accumulation of words will not show you what it is like. Too many words trying to describe a small detail or a momentary glance will only destroy the image. I could easily write paragraphs in tender praise of that young girl's pouting lower lip, but the end result would be to make her appear ludicrously deformed. An hour's work with a fine brush might, just might, manage to get an approximation of the vividly human colour, softness, fullness, femininity, innocence and yet sensuality of that one small feature of her beautiful face.

She was an entrancing creature, pale and dark-haired and naturally elegant. Her slender body was untidily bundled up in a big leathery jacket and she was wearing long, shiny red boots. But even under this camouflage of contemporary tat you still had the strongest impression that her limbs were as lovely as her face. She was not a garish poster girl or the kind of woman you see on magazine covers, shellacked into book-stall anonymity, but she was much closer to that real yet elusive image those boringly and indeed obscenely ubiquitous categories of commerce keep striving so unsuccessfully to represent. That is, her grace was totally unconscious, deva-statingly so, movingly unattainable. Her femininity was ex-pressed in the slightest tilt of her dark head or the most incon-siderable movement of her shiny boots beneath the table. Any normal man would find it a pleasure just to sit still and look at her, drinking her in.

At first her companions did all the talking. The two rowdy West Indians obviously thought of themselves as wits of the first order and they were able to make the fat lady respond to their nonsenses with weird bursts of laughter. A sound more like a furry animal in pain than a big white woman enjoying herself.

One of the brown immigrants deliberately poured some of his coffee over the pale slab of sugar crusted fruit pie he was eating, and this was thought to be a brilliant piece of impro-vised humour. The fat lady shrieked and the two Caribbeans twitched their long, loose limbs, delighted with themselves. But the girl smiled faintly, almost aloof, perhaps even disap-proving.

As I write this I realize at last why it is that her face has kept coming to me in this room. She must have reminded me in her remote stillness, her lucid silence, of someone I used to know, used to love. I have again the impression of a girl, another girl, sitting still and silent in a crowded room at Oxford while everyone else's meaningless chatter bumped around the walls or dropped like limp catkins on to the wood-block floor.

Oh, where are you? Why have you abandoned me?

Perhaps I should write her a letter. Perhaps she will read this book and at last understand what I tried so hard to tell to

78

her. Perhaps she will once more reach out with those long hands to –

No! This is ridiculous! One might as well expect mercy from a killer shark or warmth from a cube of ice. Blow, blow, thou winter wind. This room is as cold as a cabin in the frozen woods, but it is not so cold as the heart of the person to whom I gave my love, my hope, my talent. Everything now is set in ice, mast-high, floating by, as green as emerald, as green as her eyes.

> The ice was here, the ice was there,
> The ice was all around:
> It cracked and growled, and roared and howled,
> Like noises in a swound!

But this incantation I use does not calm me any more. The old man with the skinny hand and glittering eye, the ancient mariner, was telling his tale in the past tense. 'The ice *was* here, the ice *was* there, the ice *was* all around.' Wedding guests and others on the way to whatever feast are not so ready to listen to distress in the present tense. Yet for me the ice *is* here, the ice *is* there, the ice *is* all around. It cracks and growls, and roars and howls, like noises in a swound. Or noises on the telephone.

'You've got all that additional tension which readers are bound to recognize,' he said this morning, this very morning. 'The way you weave in your own background, your own illness, and that trouble or guilt Robert was trying to tell me about . . .'

The danger of writing when you are abnormally tired – as well as bitterly cold – is that you can too easily lose control by digressing too far from the important things that need to be expressed free of any other clutter. Shivering at the table and peering down at the paper under the stumpy candle I allowed myself to wander off the straight path through the dark trees.

But yet again instinct, or something even more mysterious, has sent up (or down) that warning pulse which jerks me back into wary consciousness. Again the voice on the phone seemed to be directly in my ear. Again, as in the coffee bar, I almost turned round, so clear was the tone, so near.

Perhaps – though I hardly dare pen the thought – perhaps, perhaps I am beginning to glimpse or sense out of this pain and this cold and this exhaustion and this fear and this hunger the presence or the comfort of some other thing, some other force more powerful or resilient than my own weakening frame. But I hardly dare think it. I fear to acknowledge it.

And yet I am alert again. I am peculiarly refreshed. I can tackle the central issue, head on.

Women. They are the root or the flesh of the problem. It is my attitude to women, or my conduct with them, which provides the rumours, the poison, the imprisonment in an icy room. Women. That is what Robert and my agent are on about. That is what the conspiracy is made of. That is why the couple whisper and point to me on the bridge. That is why the gutless time-servers at the Polytechnic asked me to leave. That is why the man with binoculars stands on the opposite side of the road. That is why I should never have delivered up the opening pages of my long-worked novel to that ten-per-cent moron with the art-school mind and barrack-room mouth. Women, women, women!

All right, then. Let me be explicit. Let me give examples. Cast your mind back to my description of the girl in the coffee bar, the one I gazed at earlier on in this long night, the coldest night of the year. She is the last woman I saw. And she can stand as an example of all my attitudes or of every other encounter with the female sex. She is still in my mind and so I can be totally accurate in recording my responses and in describing what took place. I can see now that she is a blessing in red-booted disguise. It is as though she was deliberately coaxed into that warm and shabby coffee bar by whatever saving force or spirit I can feel ever more strongly in this no longer quite so bleak habitation of mine.

I have already tried to describe her beauty. The words I used may strike you as generous, or too romantic, but they are not inaccurate, merely inadequate. I would find the same difficulty in putting down words for a dragonfly above a summer pond or a new spider's web hung with dew on a spring hedgerow. I gazed at her for a long time, slowly enraptured. Something about her, some innate grace, moved me deeply. The tables and the chairs, the cups and the spoons, the stains on the wall, the dust on the floor, the ache in my mind – all these things and everything else in sight mercifully receded for whole minutes at a time as my eyes took in the picture of that girl with the black hair, the pale face and the red boots.

My response was one of humility. I did not want to touch her. I had no intention of speaking to her or signalling to her. I simply wanted to gaze, and to pay my silent respect.

This person, I thought, is what a woman *should* look like: this figure sitting opposite me with food and drink and companions manages to represent without acquired coquetry or self-diminishing selfconsciousness the very essence of femininity, the quality bestowed in at least some measure upon mother, sister, wife, daughter, the power which in its apparent passivity is most naturally creative and dynamic, the sweetness which belongs to the rhythms of earth and moon and song and dance, the ideal which tempers the brutishness and vulgarity and wanton egotism of man as he plunders our planet, napalms distant villages, pollutes the great oceans and corrupts every healing dream that has ever been wrenched by noble minds out of the bleak absurdities of this brief and cruel existence.

Who would want to soil such a figure? Who could be so abominable and so foul and so devoid of proper awe that he might heave and push and grunt and pant above her parted legs? Surely not Casanova himself!

I am disgusted by the thought of spoiled human flesh. Mouth upon mouth, tongue against tongue, limb upon limb, skin rubbing at skin. Faces contort and organs spurt out a smelly stain, a sticky betrayal. The crudest joke against the human race lies in that sweaty farce by which we are first formed and given life. No wonder we carry about with us a sense of inescapable loss, a burden of original sin, and a propensity to wild, anguished violence. We cannot and never will understand this place appointed for our second race, for we are implicated without choice in the catastrophe of the copulations which splatter us into existence. We are spat out of fevered loins, or punctured rubber, or drunken grapplings in creaking beds.

But none of this disturbed my mind or my body as I looked across at the girl in the coffee bar. She was not the whore who lurks under the demure exterior of even the most respectable wife and mother. She was not an angel capable of mutating into a writhing, biting snake on a soft mattress. To me, at that moment, she was instead the Snow Queen, the Snow White in the glass case, the Princess at the ball.

Yes, I can adore women. Yes, it is a holy impulse in me to worship and to cherish them. I would like to bring them flowers and round boxes of Turkish Delight and strings of beaded sea-shells. I would write letters glowing with warmth and tenderness, poems as though to a damsel with a dulcimer, gentle cadences for gentle ladies with eyes like emerald. Indeed, I have in the past done so, filling pages of foolscap paper with words spangled as wildflower, natural and sweet. Some of my best writing has been lost in this way, for I have reason to suppose that the letters were not kept, not even in an old shoe-box. It does not matter.

What *does* matter is that this attitude, this adoration, this genuine sense of awe and gentle, honourable *respect* for womanhood should be placed on record as an accurate indication of my state of mind and pattern of conduct. If you balance the filth of the rumours or the sly hints and obnoxious asides of people like Robert and my agent against the decent, if romantic, dignities shown in the preceding paragraph and again in the portrayal of the girl I saw earlier on this night you can surely be left in no doubt as to where the weight of the truth falls.

How could a man who feels as I do, who writes what I have written, behave towards a woman – any woman – in ways remotely akin to the ones which have been suggested?

How could such a soul as I have fornicated with one single prostitute, let alone have repeated the grotesque abomination *another one hundred and fifty-five times!*

Imagine exactly what this would involve. Think and think again of the number of different rooms, the multitude of different beds, the mirrors, the endless dark stairways, the duplicated obscenities, the handfuls of folded pound notes, the sordid exchanges in doorways or park benches, the varied postures of so many unclean and degraded females spread-eagling themselves for lucre, the bodily smells, the cheap perfumes, the wasted seed, the anxieties about disease, the fears of recognition and the intolerable pressure of guilt that would inevitably descend like a black mantle over even the most vulgar and sensual head.

When you have thought about all these things, when you have fully absorbed into the darkest parts of your mind the sub-human horror of them, you will realize, must realize, with the blinding force of a revelation that I could not by the very nature of my soul be so implicated in such a maze of lust and filth. I could not have done these things any more than I could have killed my mother.

I am not a virgin, but I try to keep myself pure and I always keep my body clean. I will not listen to dirty jokes in a public house. I do not leer at the advertisements along the underground escalators. I do not possess any pornographic publications or pictures of couples in lubricious postures, though I am aware that they exist to an ever more proliferating degree, and I have seen these things in Robert's room and in my agent's office. The two people, in fact, who lead the campaign against me!

Obviously, they are by doing this attempting to discharge their own guilts, hide their own feverish obscenities, evade their own personal responsibilities and cleverly avoid gossip or rumour which would be more lethally accurate than that which they have generated themselves. The world belongs to the cunning, and fortune drops like golden apples into the laps of the unscrupulous. You only have to look around to assent to the truth of this bitter observation: contamination is the norm, corruption is the accepted social lubricant, deceit the everyday fuel, whether in the intimacy of personal relationships or in the public arena of the affairs of state. In this society it follows that real talent goes unrewarded and unflinching purity of soul is automatically derided – on both these counts I am to be numbered among the punished, especially in regard to material goods and services, financial security, the trust and love of friendship, and the divinely counselled companionship of wife and family.

Yet too much can be made of these awards and rewards, these comforts and passing benefits. It is how you regard yourself, by what standard, which is far more to the point. Hazlitt, facing death, was still able to say, proudly, that his last hopes or ideals were also his first ones. Betrayed by that slut Sarah Walker who was once his landlord's daughter, plunged into crippling debt, mocked by polite society and dinner-table assassins, tortured by a cancer of the stomach, he could still prop himself up on one elbow in a room as shabby as this one and say exultantly 'Well, I've had a happy life!'

His trouble was that he drank far too much strong tea and so ruined his digestive system. We can therefore discount his dyspeptic remarks about Coleridge being an apostate. I am sure that I would have got on with both men, famously well. Oh, how puny my contemporaries seem by comparison! Yet these are the lice and the slugs who sit in judgement on me, the trendy, shallow-minded, illiterate time-servers, the Giffords of our time, who can destroy reputations, dishearten the innovators, bully the imaginative, slander the pure, cheat the innocent, mock the talented and sully the cleanest of spirits. They can thank whatever devils they happen to worship that I have much gentleness in my soul and am not given to vituperation or excessive polemic.

Nor do I care for gossip. I have no desire to pass on nasty stories about other people, not even when I know the facts of the case. I did not even complain to the British Medical Association – as I was in law entitled so to do – about the gross impertinence of a certain toothy and incompetent doctor in this very borough who imagined in his stupidity that I was incapable of reading upside-down the notes he was making on the other side of a desk at which I was once unwise enough to sit. I do not make a fuss, I do not rant and splutter. I simply remove myself, calmly, and with a dignity that must be noticed even by those who would have to look the word up in a dictionary to get some faint glimmer of an idea of what the concept actually means.

But a distaste for gossip should not be construed as a total reluctance to express the truth about another person's behaviour when no possible alternative exists as a way of defending myself. And so, however unwillingly, and before I return to the dark-haired girl in the coffee bar, I feel obliged to describe now an almost incredible tale about my former friend Robert.

In normal circumstances, of course, I would not dream of doing this. I would be content to keep the events locked away in my head, if only out of plain charity, or respect for those other characteristics of the person in question which to some extent balance or even explain the apparent iniquities of his behaviour. I do not wish to be like those dumpy, chisel-faced women with shopping baskets who tut-tut scandals to each other between the stacked shelves of dog-food, striped toothpaste, coloured toilet-rolls and instant mashed potato in the supermarket opposite the triangle of Shepherd's Bush Green.

I have just one cigarette left. I have also been at work for eighteen hours in an icy room with one thin sandwich and one wretched cup of coffee to sustain me. In this long, cold day and night I have managed by a great, indeed gargantuan, effort to write seventeen thousand five hundred and eighty-one words. I propose, therefore, to enjoy this last cigarette, warm my hands above the stumpy candle, and think with due care and compassion about the true story I have to relate. I shall have to write in small letters as my pile of paper has considerably diminished, but write it I must.

Strangely enough I no longer feel especially weary. I do not feel quite so cold, either. It must be nearly dawn, for there are more traffic noises breaking into the darkness outside.

And I am still aware, gratefully aware, of the as yet undefined and perhaps indefinable presence of something greater than or beyond myself and my body, something sustaining me, feeding me, encouraging me. There is another source of light between these walls, a light which cannot flicker and die like that from the misshapen lump of white wax dripping into the saucer on my table.

The candle will light my cigarette, though. Let us relax, then. Let us blow smoke at each other, you and I.

A long way from here the amiable and taggled sheep are still curling together in the roadside bus shelter and the wind still moves through the unclad trees. In about an hour, I suppose, it will be dawn there, too. A faint glow of orange pushing through the stalky horizon. Before I light up, or as I was about to light up, I think suddenly of Daniel Miller.

He must, of course, be stuck on the page where I left him. If he were not a mere creature of my mind I imagine he would by now have fallen into a dangerous sleep of despair and exhaustion, frozen in a little car outside a small cottage he is too fearful to enter. He counts empty numbers while I count words, real words.

I must admit that for almost the first time I feel a stab of concern for him, a gesture of fellow regard. Since he can do nothing unless I write it down I think that before I light this last cigarette of mine I will let him go into the cottage. I will even put a bed there, in the corner beneath the small window. He can sleep. He will not freeze to death. I do not lack mercy.

But now it really is time to drop this pen out of my stiffening hand. Let us relax, please. Let us blow smoke at each other, you and I. Smoke gets in your eyes, your green eyes, my icy love.

I hope *I* do not fall asleep. I dare not do that. Not yet. Not yet. But I do not think I have to worry about it – there is, oh there is, there really is, another kind of light between these walls, too luminous for words. Emerald?

No, I do not wish to give any sort of name to it because I do not yet grasp the true meaning of this 'presence': all that I sense, however vaguely, is that it or he or He is *not hostile*.

'God bless and protect you, friend, brother, beloved!'

PART OF A LETTER, OF LATER SIGNIFICANCE

To Thomas Poole. Saturday night, November 5, 1796.

Thanks, my heart's warm thanks to you, my beloved friend, for your tender letter! Indeed, I did not deserve so kind a one, but by this time you have received my last.

To live in a beautiful country, and to enure myself as much as possible to the labour of the field, have been for this year past my dream of the day, my sigh at midnight. But to enjoy these blessings *near* you, to see you daily, to tell you all my thoughts in their first birth, and to hear yours, to be mingling identities with you as it were, – the vision-wearing fancy has indeed often pictured such things, but hope never dared whisper a promise. Disappointment! Disappointment! dash not from my trembling hand the bowl which almost touches my lips. Envy me not this immortal draught, and I will forgive thee all thy persecutions. Forgive thee! Impious! *I will bless thee*, black-vested minister of optimism, stern pioneer of happiness! Thou hast been '*the cloud*' before me from the day that I left the flesh-pots of Egypt, and was led through the way of the wilderness – the cloud that hast been guiding me to a land flowing with milk and honey – the milk of innocence, the honey of friendship!

I wanted such a letter as yours, for I am very unwell. On Wednesday night I was seized with an intolerable pain from my right temple to the tip of my right shoulder, including my right eye, cheek, and jaw, and that side of the throat. I was nearly frantic, and ran about the house naked, endeavouring by every means to excite sensations in different parts of my body, and so to weaken the enemy by creating division. It continued from one in the morning till half past five, and left me pale and fainting. It came on fitfully, but not so violently, several times on Thursday, and began severer threats towards night; but I took between sixty and seventy drops of laudanum, and *sopped* the Cerberus, just as his mouth began to open. On Friday it only *niggled*, as if the chief had departed from a conquered place, and merely left a small garrison behind, or as if he had evacuated the Corsica, and a few straggling pains only remained. But *this morning* he returned in full force, and his name is Legion. Giant-fiend of a hundred hands, with a shower of arrowy death-pangs he transpierced me, and then he became a wolf, and lay a-gnawing at my bones! I am not mad, most noble Festus, but in sober sadness I have suffered this day more bodily pain than I had before a conception of. My right cheek has certainly been placed with admirable exactness under the focus of some invisible burning-glass, which concentrated all the rays of a Tartarean sun. My medical attendant decided it to be altogether nervous, and that it originates either in severe application, or excessive anxiety. My beloved Poole! in excessive anxiety, I believe it might originate. I have a blister under my right ear, and I take twenty-five drops of laudanum every five hours, the ease and *spirits* gained by which have enabled me to write you this flighty but not exaggerated account. With a gloomy wantonness of imagination I had been coquetting with the hideous *possibles* of disappointment. I drank fears like wormwood, yea, made myself drunken with bitterness; for my ever-shaping and distrustful mind still mingled gall-drops, till out of the cup of hope I almost *poisoned* myself with despair . . .

I am anxious beyond measure to be in the country as soon as possible . . .

Write to me all things about yourself. Where I cannot advise I can condole and communicate, which doubles joy, halves sorrow.

God bless and protect you, friend, brother, beloved!

S. T. Coleridge.

PART THREE

ONE SORT OF ENDING

When he woke up, chilled and stiff, he could not at first understand where on earth he was nor where he had come from. For a moment he was not even sure who he was supposed to be. His eyes swivelled in an old panic, trying to look inwards.

An insipid winter light dribbled in a thin gruel from a small pane of glass set low in the wall just above the camp bed on which he sprawled. The rest of the room was barren of any furniture. The bed itself had an old, lumpy mattress which gave off a faint odour of damp or rotting fabric – or perhaps it was the lingering smell of sheep.

He lay still for a while, steadying himself, waiting for explanations to arrange themselves in his head.

'The Forest!' he said, sitting up with a sudden movement.

The long car-ride through the cold night woods flowed back into his mind. He remembered that he had been lost, apparently going round and round the same spiralling loop of bumpy and frozen track. He remembered the hostile trees, the rain and the fear. He remembered the lights of the car at last picking out the yearned-for shape of the cottage. He remembered the exultation of that dazzle, and then the disappointment, and then the despair, and then his own voice gabbling numbers, and then the oblivion.

But what had happened after that?

He had no recollection of leaving the car. He did not know how he had got the door to this place to open. He could not recall lurching like a drunk across the small room and throwing himself in a gibbering heap upon the bed. He could not bring back any coherent dream from out of the hours which followed.

The only impressions from his heavy sleep which touched him with a faintest trace were mysteriously, elusively compounded of plumed candle flame, drumming rain, a ship held by ice, huddled sheep, and a malignant shadow stooped muttering over a desk or table or bench in a room or a cell he thought he might have been able to recognize if only he could have opened his eyes.

He searched deeper, trying to pull up more substantial impressions to the choppy surface. He tensed his body, as though anticipating a blow.

But something had changed. The parameters of his being had shifted. He wanted to grasp the newness, or to measure it in some way, hardly daring to hope that it was good.

'Lucy?' he said, as his own name returned.

No, she was not involved in this. She was certainly not here. Best not to think of her now, best not to call out for her.

Carefully, he flexed his bent fingers. They tingled unpleasantly. He put his feet on to the floor and saw that he still had his shoes on.

He gazed slowly around the bare little room, puzzled, shivering, sore, wanting to speak, and trying to hope.

And then he knew that he was entitled to hope. The change *was* good.

A pressure had lifted in the night. An oppression had gone. It did not matter now that he was stiff, itching, cold, and dry-mouthed with hunger. These were trivial afflictions compared with the burden which had disappeared, gone like the flapping black wings of carrion crow that had gorged enough on the dead flesh in the field.

Daniel sat on the bed and clasped his hands against the sides of his head. He needed to feel the bones of his skull, wanted to explore the contours of his brain cells. It was as though he had taken a drug, not one to make him hallucinate but one to end hallucination.

The Author was gone?

'The Author?' Daniel asked, out loud, and with incredulity.

Yesterday he had thought of himself as a character in an obscene novel. In the car he had seen himself in words on a page, a helpless being pinioned by letters, manipulated by a creative intelligence that seemed set upon punishment and pain rather than any grace or redemption.

'Can any hide himself in secret places that I shall not see him? saith the Lord. Do not I fill heaven and earth?'

The old phrase from a chapel childhood sprang at him, whole, and complete with the smell of daffodils in stale water in the chapel windowsills, the musty scent of Sankey's Book of Sacred Songs and Solos, the fat lady at the harmonium, the long ah-men of Sunday mornings, Sunday afternoons and Sunday evenings.

'Can any hide himself in secret places that I shall not see him?'

This was how he had felt, yesterday, the days before yesterday, and intermittently in all the thousands of days since childhood. Once it had been the God who was supposed to have asked that too familiar question. The God he had seen, or half seen, while riding a tricycle down the long cobbled road which passed the house where he had been born. The God who had made him get off the trike and stand still at the side of the grassily banked hill.

But then God had disappeared.

In His place, and with His power, something else had slowly congealed into transcendental existence. First of all it had been merely a sense of unease, an occasional visitor. But over the past five or six years the visits had increased and lengthened until, in the preceding few months, they had settled permanently upon his presence. And it was during this time that he had lost his wife, lost his job, lost his sense of himself as a separate human soul, and in struggle worked out the theory that he was nothing but a sick character in the hands or under the pen of a malevolent Author.

He examined his own hands, looked at his own feet, touched his own face, rubbed his own tongue against his own teeth, breathed in, breathed out. And laughed.

The Author was gone.

'The Author!' he snorted, out loud, mocking himself. It was not that he had found the one secret place where the Author could not see him. It was that he had found a place in which to discover that there was of course, of course, no such Being at all.

He was himself and he was alone. He was free. And, being free, he could be ashamed of himself. His dignity now depended on this, the shame he was prepared to experience. It filled the room and spilled out towards the fringe of trees. A February landscape.

'There is no need to be ashamed,' he said, again out loud. But he was glad that there was no mirror in this room. He did not for a while want to look at his own face. He was relieved, too, that there was no other person here, not even Lucy. He did not want to have to speak for he did not want to hear the sound of his own voice. Not for a while.

'There is no need to be ashamed,' he said to himself, getting up off the bed and making his way to the door to see what his native Forest looked like in daylight and to see what sort of world it was where a man could be free and alone and full of shame.

As he opened the door and looked out he thought he heard the squeak of a tricycle. Birds make strange noises in winter in the middle of the woods. But they are only thinking of how or where to find food and how to keep alive. The grubs and beetles try to hide themselves in secret places where none shall see them, but nevertheless there are many which are swallowed whole in one swift plunge and gobble.

PART FOUR

OAK AND ATTIC

When he woke up, chilled and stiff, he could not at first understand where on earth he was nor where he had come from. For a moment he was not even sure who he was supposed to be. His eyes swivelled in an old panic, trying to look inwards.

He sat still for a while, steadying himself, waiting for explanations to arrange themselves in his head.

He was shocked to think he had fallen asleep over the table. The candle in the saucer had burnt out, leaving a stiff white pool.

The only impressions from his heavy sleep which touched him with a faintest trace were elusively compounded of dank, dripping trees, dazzling headlights, stairways, huddled sheep, a ship held by ice mast-high, and a sick man with skin blotched with words gibbering upon a bed in a room in a house he thought he might have been able to recognize if only he could have opened his eyes.

He looked down at the scatter of handwritten pages spread all over the table, and tensed his body as though anticipating a blow.

'Robert,' he said, eventually, in a slow hiss of hatred. He had forgotten all about the character he had abandoned in the February forest, the so-named Miller.

He shuffled through the pages, his fingers stiff with cold, his eyes stinging with exhaustion. His sleep had been heavy, but had only lasted about three quarters of an hour. There were more traffic noises outside and a thin light came through the window. It was just dawn in Shepherd's Bush, and he could make out without the flame of a candle the narrow, tightly packed words crabbing across the paper.

The word 'Emerald' caught at his eyes. Emerald?

'Lucy?' he said. No, best not to think of her. Bitch. Whore. Leave her out of this, let her rot away. Don't call out her name. Don't dirty your mouth, old mate.

He continued to turn the pages in his swollen hand, and soon he found the place he wanted. This was the paragraph where he had stopped.

'But a distaste for gossip', he read, glinting with agreement, 'should not be construed as a total reluctance to express the truth about another person's behaviour when no possible alternative exists as a way of defending myself. And so, however unwillingly, and before I return to the dark-haired girl in the coffee bar, I feel obliged to describe now an almost incredible tale about my former friend Robert.'

He picked up his fluted ball pen, crossed out some words, found a clean sheet of paper and began once more to write. Fourteen words went down before he stopped, hand slackening, thoughts dipping back to the girl he had seen late last night in the coffee bar. Oh, what a beautiful creature!

Unresisting, eager even, he allowed her to soak into his imagination again. He sat where he had sat and she sat where she had sat and he stared and stared at her, eyes bright with lust.

Yet they were bright with more than lust, brighter with other kinds of desire. Thinking of the provocatively slow way she might later take off her shiny red boots, dark hair falling down over her placidly unconcerned face as she bent to remove them, thinking of the longer, slower flow of her otherwise quick young body as she discarded her clothing bit by bit and turned with a sudden smile of submission towards his already rumpled bed, he was also holding in to himself and caressing within himself the glass-cased ideal of a woman – a Princess – who could be worshipped without being touched by bonily clutching fingers, who could transform him without being stickied by any of his bodily fluids. A woman, a fair lady, who would listen to him and be moved by him, moved so much that her eyes glittered before she turned her head away in gentle acknowledgement of his sincerity and his dignity.

He had stirred the dregs of his frothy coffee with a plastic spoon and he had kept his eyes fixed tight upon her, registering the slightest movement of her limbs and the most miniscule gesture which crossed her face.

It was not long – and far quicker than he knew – before she became aware of his scrutiny and soon after sensed the unusual and possibly intimidating intensity of it. She sent one skeeteringly rapid glance across the tables at him and then, for a while, pretended to ignore his presence. He was too alert not to catch the look and he was swift enough to look down in the same instant at his cup. When he lifted his eyes towards her again he thought he was safe to continue his stare, thought she was still unaware of the nature of the examination.

He wondered how much it would cost to buy her for half an hour. She wondered how much cash he had on him, if any. The hour was late, the night was cold, the district was shabby, the coffee bar was an accepted place of trade, so neither speculation was unreasonable.

But, avidly staring, he persuaded himself into both the disappointment and the relief of recognizing that the girl

97

possessed the kind of grace or innate innocence which made it very unlikely – no, impossible! filthily impossible! – that her young breasts and thighs were commodities available for temporary hire. And she, in turn, knowingly and secretly absorbing his stare as she listened to her chattering companions, began to dismiss him as a potential client. He did not look as though he had any money in his pockets at all.

She demoted him into a mere irritant with popping eyes, a frog. He promoted her to an unattainable pedestal, a figure swathed in deep purple, a princess. Neither of them was capable of searching out any fairy-tale kink in the more drab theories of evolution which might explain how it is that a frog taken (however reluctantly) into the soft bed of a princess can be changed overnight back into a prince. They were both too old and too worn to read such nonsense, that princess, this frog.

But they remained conscious of each other. Like most human beings of whatever condition or culture who send out and receive such close scrutiny in a public place the two of them dimly sensed at one tissue-thin layer within the oldest parts of themselves that the strangely alternating processes of mutual assessment had not been entirely used up.

They did not and they could not think of themselves as remotely like a frog and a princess, yet mental shapes similar in heritage or configuration managed to creep stealthily up in between the tangles of their individual cells. It was as though they had met before, these two, on some other plain or in some other desert. Assessing and being assessed, wanting and being wanted, probing and being probed, they began (without intending it) a long, slow dance of self recognition, silently accusing each other, wordlessly accusing themselves.

One of the West Indians at the same table as the girl was cheerfully full of white rum and coca-cola. Taking up the strands of the existing conversation, and wishing to demonstrate a point, he slowly poured his coffee over his piece of pulpy apple pie with the over-elaborate air of a novice waiter serving some especial and expensive delicacy.

'Is that a sauce then?' he asked the other woman at the table, a fat woman in a fur coat.

She cackled, delighted with the queasy mixture on the plate, hot brown coffee lapping at the pale wedge of sugared pastry. It reminded her of a film she had seen years before in which a cigarette had been stubbed out in a fried egg.

'Yes. That's a sauce,' the West Indian said, answering himself and making her laugh more loudly, 'It's a fucking sauce!'

His compatriot took the pun with equal pleasure and the table was fringed with laughter. The dark-haired girl, feeling a bit sick after several drinks of whisky and dry ginger, looked away from the plate and only smiled. She decided not to eat any more of the long squishy, chocolate-coated tube she had ordered. She would probably be sick later, but there was no point in throwing up there and then. One of the fellows was paying for the éclair anyway.

She half-hooded her eyes as the room shifted on its moorings. Oh God, drink! And why was that tall, thin creep staring at her? Had they had it off before?

Her stomach churned. Whisky, dry ginger, coffee, hamburger, chocolate and cream. Something else, too. A shaft of disgust she thought she had long since escaped. Twenty-two years old, she had already lost count and lost interest in the number of men she had let penetrate her slender frame.

She burped, surreptitiously, lady-like, a nasty taste in her mouth.

'What's the matter with you, misery guts?' asked the other woman, obscurely offended.

'Piss off, Marlene,' the girl replied, mildly.

Across the room, nursing the remnants of his coffee, warming himself, the tall, thin creep was greatly impressed by the delicacy and decorum with which she had reacted to the West

99

Indian's vulgar demonstration of how to ruin a piece of pie. Her smile seemed to him to have been almost aloof, perhaps even disapproving. She was the sort of woman to whom one might bring flowers or round boxes of Turkish Delight or strings of beaded sea-shells.

He imagined himself walking up to her and presenting her with a single red rose. But that was not possible, not in this place, and not with his resources. He could hardly limp across the room and offer her a plastic spoon, especially as it had already been used.

Even so, those with grace always knew how to be graceful and she would probably understand the true meaning of the gesture. The way she tilted her head gave him access to her soul. She would instantly see that a plastic spoon proffered in open-hearted supplication and tender humility was more beautiful by far than any thorny rose or second-hand diamond given to her with a leer of anticipation.

Without moving his eyes away from her dark head he oscillated between the image of the pure lady accepting the spoon, or at least the rose, and the idea of her calling out in a thrashing orgasm of female pleasure as he spurted and spurted in ecstatic triumph on top of her. Romantic dreams and sexual callisthenics, chivalry and rape, roses and semen, chocolate boxes and contraceptives . . . but most of all, never entirely out of his embattled mind, slowly dragged the shapes of the thousands of words he had so far composed on that day and the thousands he had yet to compose by candle light through the remainder of the bitterly cold night. Words with which he hoped to defend himself against imagined conspiracies, actual confession, real guilts, and words that would too explicitly, too protestingly deny too much of the substance of his own present thoughts as he looked at the girl and his own former behaviour with many, many more of her kind.

'It isn't my fault,' he began to say to himself. But he did not finish the all-but-spoken thought, for the words were sending back an echo from his own pages, the ones now in the hands of his agent. He saw inside himself a yellow-hammer flying in a startled flutter from out of the spikes and small blooms of a gorse-bush. Panic leapt up in his breast and he swallowed the last quarter of an inch of his coffee, muddily tepid. Brandy would not have done better.

There must be some way he could clamber up out of this pit. There must be one woman in the whole world to whom he could tell the truth.

The truth?

His cup drained, he looked across at the girl again. No, he didn't want to give her a rose, or a spoon, or a baby. He wanted to tell her the truth, every known particle of it. Only someone like her would be able to receive it and only a figure like that could understand the pain of it and yet also discern, beneath the scum of the surface, the beauties and longings which eddied in a clearer or cleaner current within him. If a saint could kiss a leper then surely a girl could *listen* to a man such as he?

Listen?

The girl felt a call coming like a flaming arrow across the dingy coffee bar. She lowered her eyes, puzzled. Then she raised them again, irritated. The fellow obviously had no money. He was not even wearing a watch and he needed a shave. Why were his eyes so bright? Did he know her?

Did he come from the Forest of Dean? Had he seen her before she lived like this?

Oh, what the fuck. It didn't matter anyway. But she wished the silly sod would look at somebody or something else for a change. He was getting on her nerves. What was the matter with him? Perhaps he only wanted a cigarette, or a couple of bob for the meter. She examined him, tightening her mouth.

'She is looking at me! She has noticed!' he thought with a helpless jerk of fear.

He looked down furtively into his emptied cup. Needing to

do something, anything, he rapidly tapped the spoon against the saucer as though preoccupied with a mathematical calculation. He lacked the courage to look her full in the face. He always feared that women, beautiful women, could see too deep into him. They would recoil, or laugh with contempt. They would *know*.

She watched him tap, tap, tapping his spoon against his saucer, and then tap, tap, tapping his spoon against his cup. She observed the way his foot twitched under the table with strange flicks, as though he was trying to shake off something stuck to the sole of his shoe. She knew then that he was, after all, some kind of nut. His shoes were shabby, too.

Then she noticed the walking stick jammed up against the wall between the table and the chair, exactly as though he wanted to hide it or disown it. He was just another fucking cripple. She turned back to her companions with a sniff. Fat Marlene with the wobbling chin, laughing Clyde who could smack you across the mouth without once losing his smile, and slow, amiable Harvey who always asked the wrong questions at the wrong time and had by far the biggest prick of the many hundreds or thousands she had sucked and handled.

That bloke with the stick was still staring. God Almighty!

Cripples she knew about. Nut-cases she knew about. They were all over the place, trying to lean on you, trying to make out that they cared about what happened to you. Trying to get something for nothing.

Every other Thursday afternoon at four o'clock until about twenty past she had this bald man with the brightly striped ties and the wooden leg. He cracked jokes she didn't think were very funny. Mike, he said, call me Mike, please call me Mike. She didn't care what she called him. Winston Churchill, if he liked. Or Prince Charles. Bet they are all the same, underneath.

The bloke with the wooden leg made funny noises as he

came up the stairs. Like a creaking door, or a big walking doll. It took him four or five visits before he asked her if he could unstrap what he called his piece of timber. He made one of his jokes, something about dry-rot and woodworm. It didn't matter to her whether he kept it on or not, though she did not particularly like to see how his stump got so chafed and swollen.

'So long as your prick isn't made of wood as well!' she had said with a laugh to make him feel easy. He was a regular, after all. Two nice new fivers every time, folded neatly, given like a present.

She looked across at the half-hidden walking stick again. And, yes, he was still staring at her, that bloke with the hot eyes. She burped surreptitiously, still churning. Whisky, dry ginger and wooden legs.

'Somebody interested then, Sandra?' the fat woman asked.

'Dunno,' she answered. 'Don't think so. Looks too hard-up.'

Three pairs of eyes were about to turn and size him up. Without knowing why she hissed 'No! Don't look round!' Instead, the eyes settled on her, searching out the motive for such a protective gesture. She sniggered, defensively.

'I think he's the bashful type,' she said, by way of explanation. Smiling Clyde lifted his brows, smiling suspiciously.

'Listen, baby . . .' he began, his teeth bared.

'Piss off!' she spat, suddenly furious. He might think and act as though he owned her, but he didn't. Nobody did.

If she wanted to give it away for nothing then she would. That was what Clyde was frightened of. But she didn't do such things anyway. Certainly not for creeps like that one over there.

She was glad he had stopped tapping his spoon and flicking his foot. He had not stopped looking at her, though. Looking right through her. Get off! Get away!

'What are we sitting here for?' she asked, petulant and anxious.

'Better than nothing,' said Harvey, who never seemed to care where he was or what he was doing.

'And it's bloody cold outside, darling,' added Marlene, hitching up her fur coat.

'I don't know how youse white folks stand it,' parodied Clyde, still grinning. They all laughed, not one of them willing to step out into the coldest night of the winter.

'Brass monkeys,' said Harvey, automatically. He had never understood the old joke.

But Sandra was thinking of sheep. A picture came to her of the shaggy wanderers huddling together in the bus shelter at the top of the road where she had been born and bred.

'It's a cold old night for the animals,' she said, exactly duplicating one of her step-father's regular phrases. The other three looked at her as though she had spoken in an old and now unknown language.

'*Animals?*' asked their incredulous faces.

Sandra lit a cigarette, her hand shaking slightly. The picture and the words, her own words, had surprised her, too. She didn't feel too good at the moment. Must be the drink. Perhaps it was just as well that there didn't seem to be any extra business around tonight. Unless . . .

She looked across the room again. You never could tell, not for sure. The bloke with the stick might be one of those – what do you call them? – eccentrics. They always had money, that sort. And say what you like, she thought with a small, private smile, it *was* a cold old night for the animals.

'Tis that right enough!' her mother used to reply, usually with a ball of knitting wool on her lap and two endlessly clicking needles in her reddened hands. Her mother always agreed with everybody, at least to their faces. What sort of life was that, Sandra ruminated. Stuck in a damp old house with an earth closet at the bottom of the garden, agreeing with everybody, washing, cooking, cleaning, making the beds, scrubbing the front step. Better be dead than do that.

When Sandra was nearly fourteen her mother had suddenly grabbed hold of her by the knobbly clothes-prop in the sloping garden and delivered up the one piece of advice that had been fermenting in that already greying head for decades.

'Doosn't thou ever give it away for nothing o'butty,' she had said, urgently, in that soft Forest tongue. 'Else thee'll end up scrubbing the bloody step like me.'

'Oh, our Mam!' Sandra had replied, her face aflame.

In those days she used to blush more readily. It sometimes felt that she was blushing all the time. Even so, she didn't need Our Mam to tell her what every pretty girl knew if she had any gumption at all. Her step-father had already given her a ten-shilling note and told her to keep her mouth shut about it, mind.

'Kip tha quiet, Sandra' he had ordered, wiping himself clean with a handkerchief. 'Kip quiet or you'll be sent to prison and fed on bread and wayter. Kip quiet whatever else thou's do!'

She kept quiet. But she also remembered to ask for another ten-shilling note a week later. He had threatened to hit her. She had threatened to tell her mother. He had advanced upon her with a raised fist. She had backed up against the cupboard door and threatened to tell her headmaster. They settled for five shillings, every Friday.

In the end the fourteen-stone collier had been glad to see the back of her. She was, in the Forest phrase, nothing but 'a yup of trouble'.

There had been long, bewildering visits from the school attendance officer, from the child welfare people, the police, a probation officer, the police again, a young wife with tears and an older one with a bread knife, and the police yet again. Every young ram in the village had hung about the place, hunting for what they called a bit of moss.

Her mother had continued to knit, to cook, to scrub, to wash and to agree with everybody. But Sandra would have none of it, not ever. She wouldn't let him get near her again either. Once he had put out his hand to touch her half-exposed breasts while she was washing her long, dark hair in the big bowl on the kitchen washstand. She had turned and bitten him. When he protested or pleaded, she threw the sudsy water into his face.

He was glad when she went, taking only a carrier bag full of stockings and underclothes and not leaving a note of farewell or even any address where she might be reached.

'Her'll come to no good, ol' un,' they said in the pub. He felt ashamed of her, and he could not work out why her mother should have such a smile on her face. She seemed, for once in her life, to disagree with everybody. Without saying so, of course.

Sandra, come to no good, had not consciously thought of 'home' for a long time. Sometimes she dreamed fretfully of trees that came right up close, like gnarled old men walking, but they did not belong to any patch she recognized. They were not rooted. Occasionally she was caught for a fraction of a second with images of a pig's cot wall with a black cat on it or a square stone chapel silhouetted in Sunday dusk, but these were inconsequential visitations, debris from the past uncovered by the rhythms of a particular song or the set and angle of a passing face, a passing mood.

She had not before this night thought of the sheep in the bus shelter. Funny, the sort of things which popped into your head. Funny, the kind of things you found yourself saying sometimes. 'A cold old night for the animals.' She scraped her boots together.

Perhaps she would go back one day. In a Rolls Royce – a yellow one.

If she did, she thought with a flash of venom, she would coax her step-father back into the woodshed where she had first had it. She would smile and smile while he unbuttoned his flies, trembling and muttering those nervous endearments as he had more than eight years before. She would smile and hold it and smile and then . . .

She closed her eyes as a surge of sickness came up inside her. The disgust had been long delayed. She knew at that moment that she wanted to injure every penis that ever came into her hand.

'What's the matter, San?' the fat woman asked for about the fifth time since they had all trooped in out of the cold.

'Nothing,' she answered, flat voiced, but wanting to cry.

Chatter boiled up around her. She could hardly bear to listen to them, smiling Clyde, amiable Harvey, fat Marlene. What would they do if she burst into tears? What would the man who was still staring at her *do* if she stood up, here and now, and screamed for help?

Ach, he was only another fucking cripple!

Cripples she knew about. Nut-cases she knew about. They were all over the place, trying to lean on you, trying to make out that they cared about what happened to you. Trying to get something for nothing. Round and round it goes.

'Doosn't thou ever give it away for nothing o'butty.'

They had all paid, all the cripples and all the nut-cases. The man with the wooden leg. The man with the liver birth-mark down one side of his face. The man who told her he was Jesus Christ, second time around. The boy with six fingers on one hand. The blind one. The deaf and dumb one, who seemed about to speak or make a noise as he came. The man who wanted to do it with a cigarette in his mouth. The hare-lip. The wall-eyed one. And the fellow who told her that he was from another planet.

It didn't concern her where they came from, Marylebone or Mars. And by now she didn't care what shape they came in either, old, young, fat, thin, black, white, brown, whole or damaged. Not so long as they handed over the pound notes – though smiling Clyde took most of those, the greedy sod.

'Ain't that right Sandra?' he was asking with an emphatic flourish, a wider grin.

'Yeh,' she said, knowing it didn't matter what the question had been. The simplest and safest response was to agree with him, and then find a way of doing what you wanted later. That was why she had two bank accounts and an occasional bruise on her face.

Across the emptying room another hurt mind had been at the same moment of time glanced by unwanted evocations of shabby Forest sheep nudging together in a brick shelter on a high road through the trees. Looking at each other, wordlessly grappling, two people from the same small segment of the country had unknowingly provoked in each other ill-formed shapes of what used to be home, and as yet unrecognized images of what used to be themselves. The slow dance was quickening, swirling them back and back through the darkening woods and stabbing gorse of memory to the sheep trying to escape the cold night and, beyond that, to the ways in which each of them, Forest girl and Forest boy, had first joined body with another.

Forest boy, quick of eye, fleet of foot, but pale and spindly and pensive. One of those cowardly specimens who observably flinched in the football tackle or too noticeably avoided the sporadic playground rough and tumble. A worry-gut with too many improbable questions but also – so far as most of the forty others in his class were concerned – shamefully many of the right answers when the tough old lady with tightly bobbed hair and long blackboard pointer came stalking in squeaky lace-up boots up the narrow aisles between the desks.

A boy who used to wander off alone into the tall trees which threatened the village and, as though in insolent reminder of their dominance, sent long poking fingers of animated shrub foraging between the dumpy houses, the stone chapel and the corrugated band hut.

He once knew the trees as living beings, idiosyncratic

creatures bowing only to the wind, absolutely sovereign over their individual territories, determining the dapple of light and shade, the texture of the loam rubbed between the fingers, and even the breed, rank and colour of the underlying foliage creeping stealthily beneath their high, swaying boughs. Ferns and foxgloves, droopy-leaved sallow, buckthorn, white-beam and goat willow.

The earth thickened and made different sounds underfoot as ash gave way to elm. He learned, too, how the soil became damper and less resonant as both species gradually abdicated before the tattered white willows which marched thirstily alongside the streams that tumbled towards the river.

But for him, and most of the Foresters, it was the oak which was king. These trees clustered everywhere in dense clumps, and they were the grandest of all, arrogant and yet familiar, noisy but amiable. A good tree to climb, and magnificent as a high perch. You could set your back against the roughened old trunk, plant your feet securely on the wide bough and gaze out undisturbed over the great surges of greenery.

Up top of a proud oak, safely saddled, lulled by summer sounds and accidental thoughts of Sunday hymn, the pale ten-year-old let his mind drift off into an even leafier land not on the map. A place where the trees sang to each other in a secret tongue made for praise. The birds, bright and beautiful, dipped their wings exultantly in the lucid flow of air. Ferns and foxgloves understood the sallow. All the spreading woodland hummed and buzzed and trembled, shimmeringly alive with the knowledge of itself, aware of the presence of a protective grace moving above, beyond and yet within itself. Every leaf and twig and trail of creeper was held in a radiant harmony, at peace with all else, trilling like blackbirds.

From up here, the Forest of Dean was a holy land. The boy had entranced himself.

The Bible had always had a local topography in his imagination. The Valley of the Shadow of Death was the steep lane that dropped between darkly overhanging hedgerows a few hundred yards from his home, a stony track where one walked at night whistling. St Paul was struck by his vision on the road that passed the small saw-mills, whining blades slicing through timber. Galilee, the big tree-fringed pond by the pit where his father worked, a stretch of water ruffled by the wind when he first saw it. Wood pigeons coo-cooed, waiting. Wings smacked on water, calling.

But this experience up in the tree, the knobbled bark against his back, the leaves at his ankles, was of a different order. God was not a word in a book or a gigantic figure in the sky. He saw that God was things, was in and of things, every sort of thing, breathing through them, breathing out of them – and if you took that presence away then the things, every sort of thing, would have no colour, no movement, no smell, no sting, *no point*. There would be nothing. The world fell away below him, sucked into a chasm. Wings ceased to beat against the air. The humming and buzzing sounds of summery woods faded away into a dreadful silence, like the sudden stopping of a heavily ticking clock in a room with shrinking walls.

He almost fell out of the tree. But then the hard wood pressed notches into his back, and his whirling, emptying head steadied, filled, and put God back into the world, holiness back into the Forest. A brilliant bird alighted on the opposite branch, cocked its head to show the jewels set within it, settled, and then realized that the boy was there, a mere span away. It leapt back into the air with an explosive flutter of wing and tail, warbling consternation, signalling alarm.

The boy stared at its departing form, amazed that the bird should be so frightened. Did it not know the truth? Could it not *trust*?

Far away across the varied greens and browns the wood-jagged horizon gave way to the faint blue hump of the

Malvern Hills. In the opposite direction, firmer in outline, more clearly separated from the cling of the sky, the darker mountains of Wales set the boundary of his vision. Sitting safe in the big tree, hidden within the protective myriad of bough, branch and leaf, he was submerged in a greenish half-light filtered through layer upon layer of natural growth, and he was looking out from the dimming or dappling shelter of his high cave into the dazzle of a rare summer brightness beyond. The boy was not then aware, of course, of how frequently an idling or unanchored mind can be disturbed by the accidental experience of receiving luminous images from out of clear, sharp light when it is itself cast in any sort of shadow. It is physiologically unsettling to gaze out from a dark patch into a brighter one.

For him, at that time and in that position, everything that could be seen between the distant boundaries of blue hill and black mountain, everything that spread below him under a fathomless heaven, was resonant with new meaning, new speech, new glory. It was a total illumination.

He held on to it for as long as he could. He stayed still. He tried not to hear himself breathing. He even tried not to breathe at all.

God was out there, walking. The bushes were burning.

Way below in the foxgloved undergrowth a dry twig snapped, sharply. The nearest birds began to pitch on a higher, longer, more anxious note. Straining to listen, the boy thought he could make out the soft fall of footsteps on the snuffled ground between the trees. Someone was moving slowly across the tufted grass.

He knew from the stories he had been told in the chapel that many people in days of old had seen God or one of God's angels. He knew, too, that they had always been scared by the sight or sound of the Almighty: they were 'sore afraid', a phrase which he understood to mean that their bodies hurt because their fear was so great. His own body hurt now. He ached with the fear that God was moving through the woods, coming nearer and nearer to him, a figure with a face he could not imagine, a shining shape, brushing past the respectful fern and pressing gently on the fallen twigs.

You could not hide from God. There was no place he could not see. You could not wait for him to pass by. You could not hunch up into the tree, hugging closer to the trunk.

He knew that he would have to climb down, hand over hand, foot dangling until it got a hold, body close to the wood, face turned up and away from whatever awesome sight awaited him at the bottom of the tree.

When he reached the ground he stood facing the trunk, unwilling to turn round.

'Hell-o,' said a voice, deep, strange. Not a Forest voice.

The boy stared at the notches and gnarls in the trunk of the oak, afraid to face the voice, terrified at the prospect of looking upon the Almighty.

'What-a the matter boy,' God said, as though English was a difficult speech.

The notches and gnarls stood out like carvings on a pulpit, thrusting their beauty at him. The branches above murmured in supplication and let through a sudden, spiralling shaft of light. A twig insect just four or five inches from his clenching face moved the length of its own body and then stiffened, a tiny creature in prayer. He tensed himself, joyful and afraid, preparing to turn, bow his head and then drop to his knees in proper adoration.

> *God is here, and that to bless us*
> *With the spirit's quickening power . . .*

Chapel voices, in full song. Now he was going to know exactly what they meant. When he turned round, he would see the shower of blessing, receive the quickening power.

Behind him the grass slithered quietly, and he closed his eyes. He could hear breathing, slow and heavy, the sweet breath of God, which made all things come alive.

A hand came down upon his shoulder and he opened his eyes again.

'You with anybody?' asked the voice, a soft purr of gentleness in it.

'No,' the boy said, whispering.

'You wanta see nice ring?'

'Pardon?' He was surprised by the question.

'You with anybody?' came the voice again, more insistent, closer to his ear.

'No,' he replied, puzzled.

'What you do here?' in caressing words, too slow and too alien.

Something was wrong. He turned, bewildered, and saw a big man with spiky grey hair, a tanned skin and eyes that later always seemed to be the colour of phlegm.

'But you're not God!' he said, almost shouting, relieved and disappointed.

The big man took half a pace back.

'God?' he said, momentarily alarmed.

They looked at each other, without moving. They were alone in the middle of acres of oak, hundreds of yards away from the nearest path. It would have been a sensible place in which to have encountered a loving creator, but it was a wretched spot for a pale and spindly child to fall victim to the predatory hunger of an Italian prisoner of war with a tobacco tin filled with metal rings made in the camp workshop three miles away across the woods.

'You with anybody?' the Italian demanded again. As he spoke his eyes were darting around and between the trees, seeking their own answer.

The change of tone, the expression in the eyes, the stance of the man communicated a threat to the boy. His mind had been prepared for an impossible radiance and it had taken time to absorb a new set of signals.

'Yes,' he said, backing up against the tree. 'I – I'm playing hide and seek.'

'Hide and seek?' The accent made it sound a strange new game.

'But I've got to go now,' the boy said, feeling the trunk pressing into his back again.

The Italian took the tobacco tin out of the pocket of his grey-green uniform, smiling ingratiatingly.

'You wanta nice ring?' he asked, stepping closer, spreading his arms.

Ready to bolt, the boy hesitated instead. The flat, oblong tin was full of chunky rings, as dull as lead but interestingly shaped and bevilled. The Italian rattled them together, temptingly.

'Nice rings,' he hissed. 'Ver' nice rings.'

'Can I have one, then? For nothing?' the boy asked.

'Sure. Sure,' the big man said, softly. He rattled the tin again, less vigorously. His mouth was wet and his eyes were still flicking from side to side.

'No! Don't want one!'

But as he tried to run, obscurely aware of danger, the Italian grabbed him. The boy fought wildly for a few seconds but then his right arm was bent back behind him until he called out in the most desperate agony he had ever known. A large hand smacked into his mouth and although he bit at it the thumb was forced like a gag between his teeth.

'Good boy,' the big man kept saying as he forced him down on to his knees. 'Good boy. Good boy. Good boy.'

The rings had spilled out of the tin and lay in the tufty bits of grass like slugs trying to eat their own tails. One of them was less than an inch away from his eye as he lay buckled up on the ground beneath the tree. The thumb went out of his mouth, leaving behind the taste of blood from his injured tongue. He did not call out again, but only whimpered.

'Good boy,' the Italian said for the last time, thickly, breathless.

Forest boy, like Forest girl, had found out too soon about the predatory appetites of the fully grown. A tin of rings and a ten shilling note, a woodshed and an oak tree, an innocence never to be reclaimed, a shock which changed even the ways of looking at the ferns and foxgloves, droopy-leaved sallow, buckthorn, white-beam and goat willow. Both of them now had images of sheltering sheep in their heads.

He was still gazing at her across the warm fug of the coffee bar. Everyone else had gone back out into the cold night air, except her three companions and the proprietor. She looked back at him, but this time he did not lower his eyes or tap his spoon against his empty cup. Fear spurted up into his mouth but he managed to hold the gaze, eye to eye.

He tried to smile at her. About to return it, she frowned instead and turned back to her talkative friends.

His foot twitched under the table and he began to play with his spoon again. The proprietor sighed and looked at his watch. Didn't they have homes to go to, these people?

There's no place like Home, provided you can make up your mind where on earth that place is supposed to be. Only the proprietor of the six left in the room had a clear idea of what the concept meant. When he bolted the door, pulled down the shutter, put the chairs on the tables, emptied the till and swept the floor he was able to walk through to the back, climb the stairs, sprawl into a big armchair and look at his collection of pictures, news cuttings, fan club items, record sleeves and signed photographs of Shirley Temple. His coffee bar was called The Lollipop in tribute to the good ship rather than in acknowledgement of any goodies for sale within.

He looked at his watch again, ostentatiously.

Harvey the conformist was the first of the five remaining customers to pick up the outsize gesture. The amiable West Indian realized that the man who served up the frothy coffee was not looking at his watch in order to see what time it was but more to indicate that he knew damned well what time it was – late, too late.

'Let's split,' Harvey said.

They all more or less agreed above undercurrents of mutual ill-will that it was time to be hit by the brutish cold again. Sandra glanced swiftly at the man with the stick, wondering what he had in his pockets. You never knew for sure . . .

One item, at least, would have been familiar to her: a folded booklet of pornographic pictures, printed in Denmark. But there were no pound notes in his wallet. Instead, he had a blue card telling him to be at the hospital for his first appointment with a National Health psychotherapist, a photograph of a fair-haired woman with green eyes, a driving licence, a library ticket, a yellowed old newspaper cutting about a forgotten murder, and a much fresher, more succint bit of print torn from last Sunday's newspaper:

TO LET unf. on ann. lease, renewable. Isolated, unmodernized but sound cottage Forest of Dean. 3 rooms. K. No tel. No elec. Built 1735. Details, map, tenders etc. Crown Commission Office, Coleford, Glos.

As they clustered at the door, preparing their faces for the raw air, she still sensed those eyes burning into her. Buttoning her coat, she glared back.

'What the fucking hell are you staring at?' she intended to say.

But even as the insult shaped itself in her larynx she discovered that she had smiled at him, openly, quickly, but unmistakably warm. An invitation that had nothing to do with money, but owed more to sheep in a shelter on the other side of England. When her red boots stepped on to the pavement the shock which smacked into her was conveniently attributed to the cold. But as Clyde touched her arm at the elbow, a gesture both proprietorial and questioning, she shook him off with a mouthful of venomous obscenities. He let his long arm hang at his side, his fist slowly clenching and unclenching independent of his smile.

The earlier smile, Sandra's smile, lingered in the coffee bar until the proprietor began to bang the chairs upside down on to the tables, impatient to spend half an hour with Shirley Temple. His last customer took the smile with him as he unwillingly left the warm room and limped back with chattering teeth to the unwelcoming flat at the top of the stone stairs. And the same smile had made him put down his pen after his brief, troubled sleep.

He was entranced by all that he thought it meant, the warm curve of young lips, the gentle gleam of understanding in the steady eyes. If only he had talked to her! If only he had called out before the door slammed shut!

Flipping back through the pile of loose pages again, he looked for the words he had written about the dark-haired princess who had so generously, so openly acknowledged his presence, the girl to whom (surely) he would have been able to tell The Truth.

Here it was. He noticed that the ink was blacker, showing how each word had been pressed hard on to the paper. A chisel on stone.

'This person, I thought, is what a woman *should* look like: this figure sitting opposite me with food and drink and companions manages to represent without acquired coquetry or self-diminishing self-consciousness the very essence of femininity, the quality bestowed in at least some measure upon mother, sister, wife, daughter, the power which in its apparent passivity is most naturally creative and dynamic, the sweetness which belongs to the rhythms of earth and moon and song and dance, the ideal which tempers the brutishness and vulgarity and wanton egotism of man as he plunders our planet, napalms distant villages, pollutes the great oceans and corrupts every healing dream that has ever been wrenched by noble minds out of the bleak absurdities of this brief and cruel existence. Who would want to soil such a figure? Who would be so abominable and so foul and so devoid of proper awe that he might heave and push and grunt and pant above her parted legs?——'

He considered, as he read, that no one would know that his penis had begun to lift when he was half way through the writing of the paragraph. By the time he had reached 'Who would want to soil such a figure?' he was experiencing a full erection. The next sentence was written in a writhe of desire, one hand already beginning a masturbatory stroke.

'Who could be so abominable and so foul and so devoid of proper awe that he might heave and push and grunt and pant above her parted legs?'

He examined the sentence carefully. Was there any change of style or tone in the next paragraph? For in between the two pages of words he had brought himself off, face stretched tight with lust, mind gurgling with images of the girl with black hair and red boots kneeling on a bed so that her full young breasts with long pink nipples dangled into his palms as he mounted her from behind, calling for her to cream, baby, cream.

After he had jerked out his desire into an already grubby handkerchief he had cried a little, sick with disgust. Looking again at the words he had written he realized that his face was once more tightening, his lips once again curling. He read on, alert.

'I am disgusted by the thought of spoiled human flesh. Mouth upon mouth, tongue against tongue, limb upon limb, skin rubbing at skin. Faces contort and organs spurt out a smelly stain, a sticky betrayal. The crudest joke against the human race lies in that sweaty farce by which we are first formed and given life. No wonder we carry about with us a sense of inescapable loss, a burden of original sin, and a propensity to wild, anguished violence. We cannot and never will understand this place appointed for our second race, for we are implicated without choice in the catastrophe of the copulations which splatter us into existence. We are spat out of fevered loins, or punctured rubber, or drunken grapplings in creaking beds.'

Yes, that could stay. Nobody would be capable of identifying the paragraph as words which were the equivalent of a man's post-coital sadness or silence. And the paragraph, composed after he had gone limp, would surely demonstrate to any reader that he, the writer, was temperamentally incapable of doing all the things he had so unwisely confessed to Robert. It was a bit extreme, perhaps, but in his present predicament the fault could be turned into a virtue. He realized that he had to watch every word, that he had to edit with great caution, crossing out, interpolating, amending. Nothing had to get through which could be used by his enemies. They already had far too much ammunition in their hands.

But he read the sentences about the girl again with an anxious expression. 'Who would want to soil such a figure?' That was not dangerous. No. But this about heaving and pushing and grunting and panting above her parted legs – wasn't it too specific, too obviously the prelude to masturbation, too explicitly the expression of strong physical yearning for her who should, in his own prose, be protected and left unsoiled?

He hesitated, reluctant to destroy any part of his own work. Then he crossed out the sentence, savagely. Black marks obliterated every word.

Peering closely at the page, though, he thought he could still make out the shapes of the words, or enough shapes to allow a quick and hostile mind to piece together the whole sentence. He scored through the lines once more, slowly and heavily. Every loop and curl was buried.

But even as he did so, he felt that the sentence, having been written, still existed on some other page. Edit, cut, amend, interpolate or transpose what he will, there is – he began to realize – a dimension beyond him which he is not now able to reach or to shift. Even if he ripped up all the pages on the table in front of him they would not be destroyed. These words were defining him, setting the limits in which he could move and the terms in which he could plead, argue or defend himself. The circle was closing.

He sat stock still, steadying himself. How could this be true?

He realized that he was tired and that he had been working too long, word upon word, hour after hour, mostly in a poor light, always in bitter cold. He knew, too, that his head had been aching and that his mind was capable of playing tricks upon him. The candlelight of the previous night had bounced too many strange shapes around the white walls of this room. Before he slipped into sleep had he not been aware of another kind of light, too luminous for words, the radiance of an un-defined, perhaps indefinable force, spirit or presence which was greater than or beyond himself? Did he not at that time, on the brink of collapse, feel something sustaining him, feeding him, encouraging him?

But once before, so many years ago, he had turned to meet God and fell into the hands of the Devil. Perhaps this room, too, was a cabin in the trees. Mocking illusions and treacherous visions of grace did not depart with the falling of the leaves.

He shuffled the pages again, trying to control the new panic or the old fear.

'The crudest joke against the human race lies in that sweaty farce by which we are first formed and given life——' the words caught his eye. He pushed the page away, feeling exposed.

The light was much clearer in this room now. Traffic noise had swollen into the full cancer of morning rush-hour. People and cars and buses were scurrying about their daily business. Another night had been defeated. It was silly to work himself into a state like this. He opened his mind to the sounds of the city.

To dwellers in a wood almost every species of tree has its voice as well as its feature: at the passing of the breeze the fir-trees sob and moan no less distinctly than they rock, the holly whistles as it battles with itself, the ash hisses amid its quiverings, the beech rustles while its flat boughs rise and fall . . .

The chair fell back with a clatter as he lurched to his feet, wanting to call out for help.

He managed to reach the window, dreading the sight he might see. If there should be trees out there, swaying in the wind, then he would know that he had lost all sense of time and place and personal identity. The effort he had put into creating another character, a Daniel Miller, would have turned in upon him and transformed him into his own words. The guilts and pains he had foisted upon a fictional being would come back in even greater strength to their source, and he knew that he would go mad.

The noises outside were definitely the sounds made by skeletonal timber in a winter wind.

He pressed his forehead against the glass. The other side of the pane was patterned in the crystalline shapes of frost. The sharp coldness pierced his skull and he opened his eyes, preparing himself for a Forest. Mercifully, the grey hulks of urban blocks emerged through the delicate tracery of window ice. In the distance two red buses passed each other. It was Shepherd's Bush, treeless, cacophonous, carbon monoxided. A big hoarding advertised a sunshine breakfast. He was sane.

And then he remembered that it was in exactly this position in exactly this place that he had turned to face Lucy, less than three weeks ago, shouting obscenities at her.

'Bitch!' he had spat. 'Dirty fucking whore!'

She had stepped back, her eyes quick with pain. He had advanced upon her with his fist clenched, wanting to kill her. Tins of rings jangled in his head.

'Get back!' she had said, arms up ready to defend herself.

But he continued to advance, for she was accusing him of going out of his mind. He had been delighted beyond speech to see her until she had nervously produced the blue hospital card from out of her handbag. She begged him to see this new doctor who, she said, was supposed to be very good, very sympathetic. The suggestion had made him go silent. She had watched him carefully, almost lovingly, as he went to the window. For at least two minutes there had been silence, and a hope grew in her. But as he turned, the dirt in his mouth, she could see that things had gone too far. She knew that he wanted to beat her to the floor.

Now, he turned back from the window again, full of grief. The thought crept into him that it would have been better if there had have been trees outside. This room in Shepherd's Bush stank of disaster. Any other place, no matter where, offered some prospect of new beginnings, some hope of self-renewal, some promise of forgetfulness. Why not the Forest of Dean?

But he was stuck here. He could not escape.

Release could only come if and when he finished his long apologia. The pages were waiting on the table. Put together, they would make his fortress.

Wearily he righted the fallen chair and sat down again, sifting through the lines of words, forcing himself to pay close attention to his own composition, the self-invented structures of his own being.

But the noises outside still seemed to him to be those of a wood in February. He was too tired to go to the window again, and did not know now what he wanted to see on the other side of the glass. Trees or buses, hoarding or dead bracken, pavements or scrub: a premonition or an intimation was coming upon him that they were all projections of an-other mind besides his own. Perhaps the whole world that he thought he was experiencing was, mysteriously, an idea in some greater head. It did not seem to be of any consequence, for it made no immediate difference. He still had to put his own words on this blank sheet in front of him.

Robert. Put the blame on Robert.

'In normal circumstances, of course,' he read out loud, testing it for credibility, 'I would not dream of doing this. I would be content to keep the events locked away in my head, if only out of plain charity, or respect for those other characteristics of the person in question which to some extent balance or even explain the apparent iniquities of his behaviour.'

He crossed out 'apparent', then read it again. The texture was right, the tone was correct. He had to keep this manner, this pained narrative, so that any reader would feel that the account had been forced out of him with great reluctance, and that the sordid events he had yet to describe were softened by the compassion and generous charity of the writer. He must be careful to avoid emotive judgements or scornful abuse. Every sentence had to be thought out in full, every adverb and adjective scrutinized for signs of contamination or hints of hysteria, those tell-tale flaws which would allow sharp minds to deduce that he was not writing about someone else's misdeeds, but his own.

His hand clenched and the pen bit hard into the paper. 'One evening in September,' he began, 'Robert found himself with nothing much to do when he had finished an afternoon lecture on the symbolism in Coleridge's dream poems——'

But Robert was an economist! He talked more readily about floating exchange rates than painted ships on painted oceans and he was as like to translate water, water everywhere and not a drop to drink into an elaborate example of the importance of adequate liquidity ratios.

Already he had given too much away. Keep Coleridge out of it. Beat off the albatross. Pull down the pleasure domes. He could not let in the faintest perfumes of incense-bearing trees in gardens bright with sinuous rills. Begin again, distant and spare, a clinical account of how a man – an economist – encountered a beautiful brown woman, the one hundred and fifty-sixth prostitute to spread herself with simulated murmurs and greedy eyes beneath his unslaked loins.

'One evening in September,' he started once more, 'Robert told me that he found himself with nothing much to do when he had finished an afternoon lecture on the international monetary crisis. His head was still chewing over the problems he had discussed with his young students at the polytechnic, but his feet – as though contemptuous of all such academic preoccupations – had taken him by chance to a long, shabby street of bow-fronted houses that had obviously known better days. There were a few trees in the street, but they were an urban stock, splotched with dirt, twisted and stunted by city poisons.'

He remembered now how soft the evening had been. The street lights had just come on, a little premature, and where they stood close to any of the orphan-like trees their electric brightness was captured in the mesh of dusty leaves, giving the street an elegance it had otherwise long since lost. Walking well that day, he did not need a stick. His skin was clear except for some roughness and a certain redness at the major joints. He felt good, and in control, free of depression and nourishingly busy in his mind. It was pleasant to stroll around on an evening such as this, thinking productively about the work which would make his name (and his fortune) and restore to him the sense of achievement he had so greatly enjoyed as an undergraduate journalist and Union wit.

'But apparently the street lights had come on and their electric glare was filtered through the torn mesh of dusty leaves, giving an elegance to the street which it had otherwise forgotten. He said he liked to stroll about on such evenings, and was scarcely aware of the place he had reached in his walk. Some dark impulse, it seems, had brought him without his knowledge to an Edwardian terrace notorious as the haunt of poor immigrants and richer prostitutes. He claims, with every semblance of sincerity, that whereas he had on previous occasions deliberately sought out these wretched and exploited females, this time he had no thoughts of fornication in his head. He was, he said, preoccupied with Keynes and not illicit copulation. In fairness to Robert, I must record that this sounded truthful.'

Walking slowly through autumn streets he had been wrestling with the ways in which it appeared to him that Coleridge had made use of a now little known book, Ridley's *Tales of the Genii*. Surely, he thought, the poet had digested passages of this work in his childhood? He had, after all, defended these lush romances of giants and magicians and genii as ways of reaching truths that were not accessible from any other track. If he had soaked this magic in as a child, then the faint outlines of Xanadu could be discerned.

The merchant Abudah is shown a prospect where the stones on the gold-dust ground are pearls, the flowers emeralds and the trees are made out of silver. All this Abudah can see by the grace of the Genius of Riches, exotic spirit of James Ridley's ornate imagination.

Abudah, Abudah, Abudah, the name jogged up and down in his mind as he passed the crumbling houses, the rusted railings, the impoverished trees and the occasional blank, black face at curtainless windows. Abudah, Abudah. He would give it a whole chapter. Gold dust sprinkled the pavements at his feet.

Abudah, Abudah, Abudah. A long way ahead of him, a young woman was walking, slowly, swinging her handbag. His senses quickened, but he still attributed it to thoughts of emerald flowers, silver trees and stones made out of pearl.

Abudah, Abudah. His own pace was slowing. His eyes gleamed, but he imagined it was still to do with the vistas shown to the merchant by the Genius of Riches. The girl in front had stopped under one of the street lamps.

Abudah saw a dome which rose to the clouds. The dome was entire gold, standing upon three hundred pillars of precious stones. As he remembered the description, the pedestal was a single ruby of gigantic proportions and everything between the pillars was carved in crystal so that the inside of the dome could be seen from any angle. Amethyst and emerald festooned the dome, topazes too, and sapphires, and emeralds, with an architrave of solid pearl.

'He was, he said, preoccupied with Keynes and not illicit copulation. In fairness to Robert, I must record that this sounded truthful. Economics has been roundly dismissed as a miserable science, and to the layman its contradictory conclusions and evident practical inabilities are more likely to provoke scorn than respect. But Robert, on that evening, was dipping back to a famous essay by the great Cambridge economist. He maintained that he was thinking about gold and the strange fascination this metal still exerts upon otherwise rational men grappling with the intricacies of international exchange rates. Gold, in short, glinted in his mind: not flesh, female flesh.'

Gold and precious stones, pillars of diamond. The vast dome Abudah had seen shone like fire in the magical landscape. Thinking of the crystal spaces, the lines of Kubla Khan unfolded naturally before him as he dawdled up the long terrace of decaying houses.

> The shadow of the dome of pleasure
> Floated midway on the waves;
> Where was heard the mingled measure
> From the fountain and the caves.
> It was a miracle of rare device,
> A sunny pleasure-dome with caves of ice!

Short enough step, that, from spaces made of pure crystal in one dome to caves of ice in another and later one. He felt excited by the jump his mind had made. A cornucopia of rare minerals leapt before him, spangled by street light as it softened through leaf. He noticed, too, the faded red and blue crescents of painted glass above the peeling doorways.

The girl up in front of him, a mere thirty or forty yards away, had a dark skin, lustrously sheened. She stood remarkably still, a peculiarly regal pose. Her legs were long and elongated further by the very high heels which she wore. Immobile, her lower limbs yet had the ripple of fined-down muscle about them, the promise of animal movement.

From spaces of crystal and caves of ice, from Abudah and Kubla Khan, from scholarly delight and childhood magic, his mind, refreshed and alert, leapt forward again. He thought of those legs gripping him, firm and yet caressing, sensual extensions of the stately pleasure-dome, sounds of silkily swishing physical delight heard in a mingled measure. There seemed nothing remotely obscene about the poetry of such a thought. It grew natural, and wholesome, out of the curiously emblemmed architrave, and the fluids of his body were liquified pearl and amethyst. He was still walking within the rhythmic pulse of an old dream, a vision that had been so wantonly interrupted by the person from Porlock.

'But whether there was gold in his mind or not, whether he was concerned with the dollar parity or not, as soon as he caught sight of the girl waiting seductively under the lamp in front of him, he fell victim to his own undisciplined and obsessive hungers. She was, as he subsequently described her, an attractive woman, in the manner of her kind. That is, the whore was pretty in a superficial way, and probably skilled in presenting her wares as temptingly as instinct allows. They exchanged what he describes, with lowered eyes, as 'the usual preliminaries', which I imagine to be a sordid discussion about the cost of one swift and surely emotionally unsatisfying and physically degrading copulation, and proceeded on their way up the now rapidly dusking street – one of them bright with the low cunning of unscrupulous greed and the other already stepping into the heavy gloom of unavoidable and deserved shame or guilt. But there was, I regret to say, much worse to follow.'

She might have been the Abyssinian maid, playing a dulcimer and singing of Mount Abora. Close to her now, and conscious of how quickly dusk had fallen, he was flooded with images, a deluge that swept ideas and impressions together in a cataract of intellectual frenzy. He was suddenly seeing right into the crystalline spaces of the famous poem. He was writing it afresh, there and then, word for word, but the words, although they were identical to the familiar text, were nevertheless *new* words, words that had not been made before.

The last smear of faded orange was being sucked out of the sky and a few windows jumped into oblongs of light along the battered terrace. Not since childhood had he been so alive to the changes of texture in the air, the shifts of mood in the sky, the beat of the blood in his own body. It was like being in the top of the oak tree again, except this time the shimmer of woodland was transformed into the dream-like rhythm of words. He could see them coming out under the hand: *And close your eyes with holy dread.*

'Hel-lo,' she said, dividing the syllables. 'Would you like a nice time, honey?'

> And close your eyes with holy dread,
> For he on honey dew hath fed,
> And drunk the milk of Paradise.

He was facing her now. She smiled, mechanically. But a film of excited, creative thought still interposed between his body and the woman, the tree, the lamp and the street before him. He stood silent, appearing to examine her, actually examining her, but plunging back beyond Coleridge to Ridley and the possible sources of the magical verse.

Abudah. Abudah.

The merchant then met the Queen of Pleasures. A boat

floats Abudah on a cool stream past hanging rocks and woods of spice towards a temple with a chest at its centre.

'It's just round the corner, love,' she said.

'How much?' he asked, still in a sort of trance, turning the brown lustre of her skin into Abyssinian maid and then the Queen of Pleasures.

'Three pounds for a short time,' she said, her voice hardening.

He brought her into focus, letting the boat drift out of mind. The perfume that had breathed sweetness over the cool stream was coming from the delicious brown girl. His body took it in, took her in, and the desire which reared in him was the strongest he had ever experienced. And still it seemed right, still it was free of the slightest tinge of shame.

'Walk behind me if you like,' she said, misunderstanding his silence.

But he touched her slender arm instead, feeling firm brown flesh beneath the loosely flowered silk of her sleeve.

'Queen of Pleasures,' he smiled, speaking as gently as a man can.

'I don't know about that,' she said. 'But I do the best I can.'

They walked away from the lamp-post and the speckled tree. He kept his hand on her arm, just above the elbow. His feet continued to pattern Ab-u-dah Ab-u-dah on the pavement as it slowly curved towards a junction with a similar, possibly even shabbier street, a terrace without any trees.

The way he was touching her and the expression in his eyes made her optimistic as she click-clacked beside him on her high heels.

'Of course you can always stay longer——' she began.

'Yes!' he said.

'If you'd like to give me ten pounds,' she added, quickly. 'I'll make it worth your while, honey.'

He did not care about the money. It was the end of the month. He wanted to give her anything, everything. Wristwatch, wallet, tie, cigarette lighter. All inadequate offerings.

'Yes!' he said again, equally emphatic.

The sight of her legs as they stretched forward to keep up with him lifted him with exultation. He was sure that she was animated by the same desire. He was going to feed on honey dew and drink the milk of Paradise.

Christ all bloody mighty, she was thinking, I've landed myself a good one here!

'You can come twice for that,' she promised, and showed him the tip of her tongue.

'Yes!' he repeated, like an idiot, tempting her to try her luck.

'And you can come in my mouth for another fiver,' she said, deliberately pushing her hip into him, letting him feel the soft flow of her limbs.

He stopped, and stared at her. She smiled, waiting. He was moved almost to tears by the sight of her. She had no past, no future. She had been magically conjured up out of dream words and dulcimer sounds and trees of spice, a creature from a pleasure-dome he had not yet seen, a Queen of Pleasures brought to life just for him, just for now. He put the tips of his fingers on her cheek, half fearing that she would disappear.

'Yes,' he said, softly. 'Yes. All right.'

'So that'll be fifteen pounds won't it?' she insisted, making sure he understood.

'Fifteen pounds?' He sounded puzzled.

'Ten pounds for a nice long time,' she said, anxiously, invitingly, 'You can take an hour if you like, honey. Ten pounds for that, eh? And another five so that you can spunk in my mouth. It'll be lovely. Ten and five. That's fifteen.'

'Fifteen,' he repeated. 'Yes. Yes, all right.'

She sighed with relief and steered him towards a gate half hanging on its rusted hinges. A short path led along cracked paving to a front door with coloured glass set into its wood. She jangled her keys.

'Here we are then,' she said.

He began to tremble as he stepped through the door and looked up at the dim stairway which climbed steeply out of the bare and musty hall.

Abudah? Abudah?

Thunder and darkness and screams. He had forgotten those. When the merchant had tried to open the chest in the temple the feasters had been blasted by lightning and some, in their madness, had torn each other into bloodied pieces. The temple collapsed, leaving only a dungeon of lust.

'Come on!' she said, irritated.

He looked up at the stairs. Abudah had to make his way through that cavern, that dungeon of lust, and the merchant was assailed now by stench and utter filth instead of sweet perfumes and woods of spices.

'I don't think I——' he began, swallowing a new taste.

Already at the foot of the stairs she whirled round, her eyes flashing in the musty gloom.

'Look, mate——!' she hissed.

But the way she had turned, quickly muscular, slim brown body lithe in its swivel, eyes big in her painted face, full lips parting in anger, knocked everything else out of his sensibilities. She was a young female animal, ready for fucking. And, yes, he had fifteen pounds in his wallet. Why not, then? Why not?

'It's O.K.,' he said, voice quavering. 'I – well, I've never paid for it before.'

He always said that in the vain hope that the girl would respond to him differently from all the others who had so casually used her body. He also liked to think that the claim was true.

'No need to be shy,' she reassured him with a professional smile. This one should be easy to get rid of, she thought. Twenty minutes at the very longest and she would be back under the street lamp.

Climbing the stair behind her, looking up at her clacking legs, his body already responding, he had turned a pillar of pearl into a hard shaft of flesh. Flowers of emerald and trees of silver decorating a ground made of powdered gold had changed in a few helpless throbs into body-crushed vegetation, stained ferns and foxgloves, droopy-leaved sallow, buckthorn, white-beam and goat willow. The treacherous oak swayed above, the tree that had promised the milk of Paradise but had stood guard instead overtop the spilling of other fluids. Precious minerals mutated into rotting vegetation.

Each step up the stairway was rank with smells. He identified the dominant one.

'Curry,' he said, behind the girl.

'It's these fucking Pakis,' she said, without anger. 'They live in all the other rooms, ten or twelve at a time.'

Abudah. For the last time. Abudah?

'Where are *you* from?'

'Guyana,' she lilted as one of the keys on her ring opened the topmost door on the last floor of the ramshackle old house. The door swung into what had once been an attic.

They stepped into a dark room. There was no space in here for the literature that had brightened his being and not enough light between these walls for fairytale merchants brought to life in old romances. And he had no idea what a dulcimer sounded like anyway. Flesh from Guyana was far more real, much more appetising, than spices from Xanadu.

The Queen of Pleasures groped at the wall and switched on the light.

'I myself cannot even begin to imagine by what mental process an educated and rational man of some sensibility moves from the reputed subtleties of Keynsian economics (the process which has, apparently, saved the capitalist system from the collapse which would in turn have provoked a revolution) to the blatant crudities of contemplating intercourse with a mindless whore. But it is not for me to moralize.

The facts are the facts, and I am compelled to record them with a plainness of detail which in the end offers the only means of extending that small degree of compassion, or perhaps even understanding, which all men in whatever circumstance or however degraded should not be denied.

'Robert told me in quiet tones and averted eyes how he climbed the stairs behind the prostitute in this house where she conducted her trade. He said that there were many doors and many smells. A strong odour of curry predominated. I can well believe that when he now catches this distinctive smell when passing Indian or Pakistani restaurants a nausea returns to him – it is, so to speak, the cuisine of shame. But this, of course, is mere speculation: I cannot inhabit his mind nor even imagine my way through the dark labyrinth of its distortions and obsessions.

'They reached the top of the stairs. The girl opened a door with a Yale key and they entered a dark room. From Robert's description of the place I presume that it had once been an attic, for it was small, the ceiling sloped, and there was no window set into the wall. The only natural light came from an extremely tiny oblong of glass in the roof, but this was so filthy, and so splattered with accumulated bird lime, that it let in the flimsiest of light. Since dusk had by now fallen, the room must have seemed almost completely blacked out.'

The Abyssinian maid groped at the wall and switched on the light. The merchant, the client, had willingly stooped into the dungeon of lust.

When Abudah had made his way through this slimy cavern he emerged upon a mountain top in the clean air. Ten thousand voices called out in praise 'Long live our sultan, whom the mountains of Tasgi have brought forth!'

Although he had been immersed for days in Ridley's exotic tale, searching out the coiling roots of Coleridge's Kubla Khan, and although he knew intellectually that so many of these stories and poems were impregnated with an unconscious symbolism which later adventures into the human psyche were to make so much more explicit, he was temperamentally incapable of seeing the hidden meaning within this laborious passing from the 'dungeon of lust' into the pellucidly clear air of the mountains of Tasgi where voices shouted in exultation. Triumphant ejaculation and healing release.

For him, the mountains of Tasgi were dank with decomposing vegetation, malodorous genitalia, fleshly betrayal, fathomless melancholy and the taste of a tongue bloodied by a thick thumb. The voices did not acclaim his deeds with a loud rapture but became whispering voices, conspiratorially accusing, viciously sniggery. Murderous ejaculation and deeper entombment.

The Queen of Pleasures was only a cruel misnomer for the Whore of Babylon. One of them switched on the light, her finger tips painted with a silvery pearl, and the other switched it off with an animal claw.

But like many articulate and intelligent people, even those trained to search out the hidden structures of literature, even those who have been moved by great art or fascinated by the most remote biographical details from the lives of writers (such as the information that Ibsen on occasion wrote with a scorpion in a jar on his desk), he nonetheless had little or no access to the springs of his own emotions. He was always surprised by joy, always surprised by disgust, always bewildered by the swing between the two.

He merely knew enough to be careful (though not careful enough) about the words coming out under his fist.

Were they safe? Was he giving anything away?

'The only natural light came from an extremely tiny oblong of glass in the roof, but this was so filthy, and so splattered with accumulated bird lime, that it let in the flimsiest of light. Since dusk had by now fallen, the room must have seemed almost completely blacked out.'

He sucked the end of his pen, wishing he had a cigarette, trying to concentrate upon these last two sentences in his account of Robert's alleged misdemeanours.

No! The detail was too specific. Robert would not have said that the fanlight was almost obliterated with bird droppings. You did not say these things in conversation, not even confessional speech. People would realize that he was writing about himself, that he had *been* in that room. It was vital that they did not think he had actually seen what he was about to say Robert had seen when the electric light flooded the converted attic.

He crossed out the sentences.

The foolscap sheets of Croxley Script ('the all purpose paper') were by now beginning to look like an inventive infant's representation of woodland scenery illicitly sketched on top of pages already thick with words. Individual adjectives and adverbs had been obliterated by a tight foliage of tangled afterthought, single sentences were submerged in blotchily leaved overgrowth, narrow black paths of muddied fear meandered between the rustling syntax, and whole paragraphs were lost beneath the heavy lattice of trunk-thick deletions. He had come now in the mid-passage of his life to a forest dark and he had lost the straight path. The words were leading him the wrong way.

He sucked at the end of his pen again, reluctant to push any deeper into the dank treescape of his own memories.

'From Robert's description of the place,' he read, 'I presume that it had once been an attic, for it was small, the ceiling sloped, and there was no window set into the wall.'

The remainder of the paragraph had been cut out. He wished that he could as easily delete the memory of what had followed after she had switched on the overhead light.

He put his pen down, flexed his fingers in a by now automatic reflex, dragged himself across to the window, looked out, and burst into tears. The hoarding across the street was still inviting any chilled onlooker to enjoy the vitamin-packed goodness of a sunshine breakfast.

'Australia,' he sobbed, forehead cracking forward against the pane. 'I'll go to Australia!'

But whether he went across the seas or not he could not pass off his own deeds under Robert's name. Some other fiction would have to be rekindled.

Fifteen minutes later he moved from the window, tore up some pages, sat looking at the scraps, and then began to write again. He was getting nearer to himself, travelling on a long loop of bumpy path through the trees.

PART FIVE

THE EDUCATION
OF CHILDREN

One evening in September Daniel found himself with nothing much to do after he had finished an afternoon lecture on the international monetary crisis. His head was still chewing over the problems he had discussed with his young students at the polytechnic. But his feet – as though contemptuous of all such academic preoccupations – had taken him by chance to a long, shabby street of bow-fronted houses which obviously had known better days. There were a few trees edging the pavement, but they were an urban stock, twisted and stunted by city poisons.

But the street lights had come on and their electric glare filtered through the dusty leaves to give an elegance to the street which it had long since forgotten. Daniel told me he liked to stroll about on such evenings, discovering these momentary beauties which accidents of light or shade or unsuspected angles of perspective brought back untarnished from former days.

This time, however, some dark impulse had brought him without his knowledge to an Edwardian terrace notorious as the haunt of prostitutes. And yet he was, he said, preoccupied with Keynes and not thinking about sex at all. He told me (and I believe him) that he was recalling the dry cadences of a famous essay by the great economist. Daniel was that evening thinking about gold and the perverse fascination this metal still exerts upon otherwise rational men as they grapple with the intricacies of international exchange rates.

But gold is not all that glisters, especially in the academic mind.

Whether Miller was concerned with the dollar parity or not, as soon as he caught sight of a young prostitute waiting seductively under a street lamp up ahead of him, he fell hapless victim to his own obsessive hungers.

Apparently, the girl was an attractive woman and she no doubt knew how to present herself as temptingly as possible. They exchanged what Miller describes as 'the usual preliminaries' about money and walked on together up the by now rapidly dusking street. It is possible to imagine that one of them was brightening with the low cunning of unscrupulous greed and that the other was already stepping into that heavy gloom of shame and guilt which could only take him to the hospital or worse.

Because I am a writer caught up willy-nilly in the polluted air of our own times, because I cannot avoid entirely the language, assumptions, behaviour and weirdly chiliastic bombast so typical of a corrupted age, I can *force myself* to imagine by what tormented mental process an educated and rational man of some sensibility moves from the cerebral subtleties of Keynsian economics to the animal crudities of purchasing unsatisfactory and momentary sexual release from a cheap little whore.

We who write have no choice but to explore the still widening dimensions of Despair. If, as Kierkegaard once claimed, *if* the whole world can be divided into those who write and those who do not write, then we are two different

138

species mauling each other without comprehension. 'Those who write represent despair, and those who read disapprove of it and believe that they have a superior wisdom.' The time is fast approaching when a more accurate division of mankind will be between those who are patients, knowing despair as well as they know the lines grooved into their own hands, and those who are psychiatrists, so helplessly and irrecoverably sick that they believe that *serenity* can be achieved by swallowing a few polychromatic biochemicals! I think, though, that this is the same separation of human categories which Kierkegaard must have meant.

Thus, it is not for me to sit in judgement upon Daniel Miller. Certainly, it is my instinct to do so. Having disciplined, explored and contained my own metaphysical anguish, having put down my own least worthy appetites, having separated myself by conscious decision from the filth and decadence of modern society, it is inevitable that my own hard-won sense of propriety or dignity should tempt me into being the scourge of other, more self-indulgent beings, fictional or not.

The temptation must be resisted as firmly and valiantly as I have resisted the other, more obvious, more sensual lures and snares.

The compassion I intend to show to Miller marks an important turning point in my own personal history. My biographers will discern a significant shift of sensibility here. They will realize, if they have any skill at all, that these last four or five hundred words represent the beginnings of a new creative period. Everything that has gone before is apprenticeship (especially the thirteen thousand words of uncharacteristically slapdash prose inadvertently handed over to a person whose only chance of later fame lies in the possibility of aspiring to the status of a footnote in the scholarly biography of my life and work which someone, even now, is probably contemplating).

Miller has of course suffered greatly. He has endured mental anguish, mind-breaking guilts and lacerating physical pain. His own conduct is a mystery to him. He will bear the scars until the day he dies, probably by his own hand in some lonely spot under a tall oak tree in the Forest of Dean. The world would be a more stable and therefore a better place if we extinguished ourselves in the same place where we first saw the light of day, and if we spent the intervening time in as small a circumference as a day's walking permits.

But I am jumping ahead of myself. The point I was making was that Miller, fictional character or not, has suffered enough without being visited by an authorial malevolence. When God subjected poor Job to grief, pain and penury He did so unjustly. Miller – were he to exist – would surely feel an equal burden if, on top of his own torment, he was further bludgeoned by the contempt and invective of his creator. Great writers, I now realize, do not do such things: if they do, they condemn themselves as well as their invented characters.

I have destroyed many pages and crossed out hundreds, no thousands, of words in order to arrive at an imaginative sympathy (though not, of course, an explicit approval) with Miller as he walks down this long, gently curving terrace of dilapidated Edwardian houses.

Ah, but it is only a story, you might say. True. But do not say it as though you know what that means, 'only a story'. Did the tale exist before I wrote it? And if it did, do I therefore know what happens, do I know 'the truth'? Do you not acknowledge your own lives to be fictions?

Those of you (few, I hope) who answer these questions in the wrong way, the stupid Philistine way, might as well close this book now and go walking about the world pretending to be real. I hope you do shut the book. I do not want to waste my time writing for silly buggers like you.

So here he is, real or not, this Daniel Miller, walking down a street at dusk with a young prostitute at his side. He did not need a stick at this time, for he was feeling better than usual, and his skin would have passed for normal except for some roughness here and there easily attributable to the chafing of clothes or to taking too many baths in hard water without the benefit of bottled body oils sold by any chemist worth the name.

The two of them arrived at the broken gate of a house even more rackety than its peeling neighbours. A short path of cracked paving led to a front door that had a crescent of dimly coloured glass set into the wood above the frame. She jangled a ring of keys, opened the door and led him up the bare, creaking stairway which climbed steeply out of the hallway.

As he went up behind her, step by step, eyes fixed on the sensuous movements of her dark young limbs, he half noticed the seemingly inordinate number of doors which opened on to the landings and he could not avoid picking up the pre-dominating odour of curry. The girl told him that the house was full of Pakistanis, and added, with a lilt of incomprehensible pride, that she herself came from Guyana. Both places had once been red on the map. The pigeons are coming home to roost.

They reached the top of the stairs. The girl opened a door with a Yale key – giving even this limited movement a lucid flow of limb – and together they stepped into a dark room. Dark because it had once been the attic of the house and its only natural light came from a tiny oblong of glass set in the sloping roof. Bird lime and other dirt obliterated the dusky light that might have made its way through this inadequate fanlight.

'Bloody hell!' exclaimed Miller, astounded by the blackness, perhaps fearful for himself, too.

'Hang on,' she said, hand groping at the wall inside the door.

When she switched on the light the little room exploded into a brightness so extreme that it hurt his eyeballs. He felt like a moth that had been sucked in to a candle flame, but the fluttering was in his chest.

'Now we can see what we're doing!' she sniggered.

There was a peculiar hissing sound in the room, a radiophonic kind of vibration, a noise one might expect on the sound-track of a science fiction film as the visiting card for the presence or arrival of aliens with long, bent, furry legs and eyes as scorching as red-hot coals.

He blinked up at the light. A naked bulb of high wattage hung on half-exposed wires from the centre of the sloping ceiling. The light was hissing. A hiss which changed into a hum.

'Fifteen pounds, you said,' she said, prepared for argument.

As he looked at her, preparing to bargain all over again, there was a splat! of sparks from the light, a high-pitched sizzle, and then darkness.

'Oh, fuck!' she said, matter of fact.

'Exposed wires——' he began, ill at ease, imagining flames.

The shapes in the room were barely discernible. But he could make out her form stretching up to the light.

'Fucking landlord,' she was saying, her hands grasping at the bulb.

'No!' he shouted. She would electrocute herself.

'Shhh!' she hissed, hands still stretched upwards in the dark. 'You'll wake the baby.'

His forehead tingled and he put his back against the door, trying to locate himself, trying to absorb what she had just said.

A splatter of sparks fell like miniature stars, the light flickered for a fraction of a second, hissed venomously and then splat again into darkness and silence. He was trembling now, his back still against the door, his eyes searching out the ill-formed contours within the room.

'Got a match?' she asked.

Yes, there were two beds in this attic. A single one of

standard size against the wall on his left, and on the opposite side, much smaller and lower, there was another hump against the wall. But surely——? No, no, surely not. No.

'Have you?' in an impatient lift.

'Pardon?' as he peered at the smaller hump.

'A match!'

He searched in his pocket and gave her a box of England's Glory. But his eyes were still fixed on the little bed, trying to make out any movement in or upon it.

The Guyanese girl struck with a hard, angry scrape and in the flare he saw that there was a child's head on a bolster at the end of the small hump. Daniel wanted to call out his shock, but the incoherent cry turned in his throat into a spurt of stomach bile. He was not looking at what the girl was doing with the match.

But then the room was filled with light and smoke. She was standing by a small chest of drawers on which were littered various pieces of domestic junk and a pile of old magazines – *True Story*, *Confessions*, *Tit-Bits* and the like. And she had set fire to one of them. *True Love* blazed in her hand. She held it up like a torch, her face expressionless.

'What are you doing!'

'Can't see,' she explained, as though it was a perfectly obvious thing to do. 'Got to fix this light, man.'

'No!' he shouted again, appalled by her stupidity.

Bits of burning paper had already fallen to the wooded floor. She stamped on them, without any sign of alarm. The magazine in her hand plumed upwards in a long flame, belching smoke. He realized that she was a mad woman, utterly mad.

'Fifteen pounds,' she repeated, dully. Then the flames licked at her fingers and she dropped what was left of *True Love* at her high-heeled feet. The pages blackened, crinkled, and curled.

'Fifteen pounds?' he asked, like a demented ventriloquist.

He was paralyzed by the sights before him. She stamped at the burning paper. She was striking another match. She was going to burn the whole place down!

He leapt at her, knocking the matches out of her hand. Red-headed England's Glory spilled across the bare boards of the floor. They stood facing each other in the murk.

'Do it in the dark, then,' she said. 'I'll fix the light after.'

'You'll kill yourself!' he whispered, his face so close to her, smelling the tawny sheen of her skin.

'One day. Maybe.' The way she spoke, all words were broken down into distinct syllables. She had hyphens at the tip of a honied tongue. The accent was resonant with a sexual rhythm.

His ears were straining to catch the sounds of a sleeping child, but his penis had stiffened again. She was standing so close to him. Her eyes shone in the gloom. Her body was drenched in what then seemed a subtle perfume, a human spice.

'Baby,' he tried to say. 'There's a baby . . .'

'Fifteen pounds, honey. You said fifteen pounds.'

'But, listen . . .?'

She stepped back, spitting like a cat.

'Fifteen!' she hissed. 'Fifteen! Or a-way you go!'

But he did not want to go. His eyes were getting used to the dim light and, as she emerged into a whole shape under the fanlight, he was more than ever conscious of how beautiful and how youthful she was. He stepped towards her, his face stretching.

She held out her hand, palm upwards. Even this gesture, a mercenary movement, had about it the lilt of broken syllables. Her fingers seemed full of an eloquent speech.

'Oh,' he stopped. 'Yes. Of course.'

As he pulled out his wallet the tautness went out of her. Every muscle relaxed. She took the three five-pound notes with a swift, submissive movement, and her body went limp.

'You can take your time, honey,' she syllabled, droopy with promise in the drawl.

'The b-baby,' he stuttered, trying to resist.

'You wanna see my bay-bee?' she said it as though she was pleased, or even flattered.

She took hold of his hand and led him over to the small bed. Her other hand had screwed the three fivers into a loose ball of paper.

'There he be,' she whispered, 'fast asleep, bless his little head.'

Barely audible, he muttered a name. It sounded like Abudah or A Buddha.

'No' she said, with a frown. 'He's called Paul.' After Newman, not the Apostle.

I do not know why Miller should have croaked out such a name. But certain words, like certain tunes, have a way of floating on the top of the mind, ready to jet out of the smallest leak in the sensibility. I can therefore understand why at that awful moment he should seek to summon up a talisman of words, a secret defence against abomination, or perhaps even an excuse in the form of some kind of precedent that a word expresses and so takes the edge of uniqueness off the contemplated evil. He was, after all, proposing to jerk up and down on top of a naked woman not more than three or four strides away from a sleeping child, her child.

How can a man do such a thing?

I have asked myself this question a thousand times, a hundred thousand times. Only by a stupendous act of imagination, only by actually putting myself in his skin in that room at that time can I even begin to attempt any sort of answer which moves by the smallest degree away from the natural responses of disgust and revulsion which all of us instinctively wish to express.

Trying to put myself in his skin in that room at that time must not, of course, be taken to mean that the act contemplated and later committed by Miller is something that I myself could think of doing. I am concerned here with the powers of my own mind, its sweep and its insight, rather than the appetites of my own body. Coleridge said that Shakespeare was 'miriadminded', but the term can also be applied to its gifted originator, too. It is this glistening miriad of impressions, moods, intuitions, intimations, dreams and visitations which I am seeking now to catch in these orderly lines of print.

And by this means, perhaps, by being ambitious or 'miriadminded', I can perhaps address myself to the nature of this foulness: *how can a man do such a thing?*

Daniel Miller leaned over the bed . . .

No. Let me be bold. Let me shift out of third-person narrative. Only by changing the tension of the text, so to speak, will we gain access to the depraved (or, at best, tormented) mind of our central character. Paradoxically the miriad-mind is the 'I' mind, the mind which does not simply observe, but *enters* into the essence of other substances or beings, be they people, animals, things or even the ghosts and spirits, angels and demons, which Reason itself has not yet driven out of the world we experience in waking and sleeping, in loving and in hating. Glory may have departed from this earth, but faint traces or soft echoes of it persist in the unlikeliest recesses of mind and landscape. Roses and orchids are too obviously beautiful, and so they lack this remnant of grace: maybe, if there *is* any harmony left for us to discover, maybe we shall as soon apprehend it in dog shit or an old man's spittle, sizzling on the grate.

Oh, my pen is singing! And it dances across the page!

These exultations, these hymns, come so suddenly upon me like unbidden genii bearing gifts that no mortals have ever seen before. Through the vapours I can even grasp at the idea that the hatred and malice of my enemies, their whisperings and pointings, are but emanations of one of the forms of love.

They value me, in fact. They respect my talent. They cherish the good in me. They will even try to understand the words I have spent so long in writing.

So let us move confidently into the first-person. The 'I' is not I, nor yet quite Miller, nor you. Just I, the writer, the God, the one who sees, who understands.

I, observing, not observed; doing, not remembering; describing, not excusing.

I leaned over the bed to look at the child. The girl let go of my hand and moved away into the gloom behind me, where she must have put the screwed-up five-pound notes on to the chest of drawers with the magazines, the small framed photograph, the towel, the box of paper tissues, the jar of Vaseline, the baby's dummy and all the other odds and ends spilled over the varnished oak top.

The boy Paul, as she had called him, was about three or four years of age, crinkle haired but almost white. Old enough, certainly, to brood upon things, and too young to make much sense of the sights and sounds he must have seen in this dismal little room. Perhaps he thought that a man, or more than one man, was trying to hurt or kill his mother, and perhaps he thought this nearly every night of his life. I felt that I was looking right into the worms of pain in his skull, but they turned into slugs trying to eat their own tails.

The light was getting better. I think the moon must have got up and a few silvery shafts were getting through the small fanlight. Either that, or my eyes had adjusted to the gloom.

My mind had not adjusted to this new sight, though. I could not move away from the child's bed. I held my breath, terrified that he might wake up. I no longer had an erection.

He was sleeping with one arm encircling his head, small podge of fingers just touching his cheek. So deeply asleep, he moved not a muscle. I was moved by the peace of him, the innocence of his head, the warm coil of his drugged limbs. I bent low over him, a sting in my eyes. I wanted to stay by this bed, protecting the child. Could he not be taken from here, still aslumber? Could he not open his eyes on a better scene, a less sordid spectacle? Oak tree, not attic.

Leaning in, choked, I saw the banner above the pulpit in the chapel I had attended so regularly as a child. My own present stance and the position of the boy in the bed must have thrown up the embroidered, tasselled triangle hanging in blue, white and gold on the chapel wall. It was a picture I had examined with attention through many an hour of boring burble, raucous revivalist song and whining, wheezing harmonium.

The banner showed a child on top of a cliff. Three or four years old, a mere toddler, a boy with golden curls gathering blue flowers. But he was perilously close to the edge of the crumbling cliff. The drop was sheer, and endless. He already had an armful of flowers, star-shaped clusters almost the same shade as the sky above. The embroidery was perfect, picking out colours of blazing simplicity. Just over the edge of the cliff the most wonderful flower of all was growing, roots and leaves out of reach on the rocky perpendicular, but the blue spangle of its bloom poking up invitingly at the jagged rim of the cliff. The boy was pictured in a stilled movement that clearly represented the brief moment before he reached out and reached down to pluck the flower, a movement which would topple him over the edge to certain death. The very stillness of the scene, the embroidered immobility of strong colours, gave the picture a complete terror. Always the boy was about to plunge over the precipice. Always the flower pulled him near, beauty tempting him in his innocence. It made you want to shout out a warning, except that the shout, too, would be pulled into the stitches, given colour, made immobile, inaudible, part of the helpless horror. This part of the banner, the lower half, was too calamitous for the eye.

But the chapel fingers had woven in the grace of salvation, the mercy of God.

148

Above the little child hovered a large angel, luminously white, with wings made to look like burnished gold. The colours glowed and deepened. The white and the gold together shone in holy radiance, and even in the stilted emphasis of embroidery the angel was watchful in its fluttering, heaven-touched thread.

You knew that as the child would, in a moment, move towards the edge of the cliff so, too, would the beautiful angel of God. The wings of burnished gold would divide the air, swifter than any fall. The boy was for ever in danger. The boy was for ever safe.

But on the long, split bench of the chapel, the floppy red book of hymns in my hands, I used to imagine every possible circumstance that might deflect the loving attention of the angel. God Himself might call it away by accident. The boy might break wind or say a naughty word and forfeit the protection of that great white spirit. The boy might have wicked thoughts, like wanting his father to die.

I half wanted him to fall, legs and arms akimbo, flowers drifting down after him. Then I would be ashamed, seeing his little body broken on the rocks below. And then, reassuring myself, I would gaze upon the white and gold protector, the messenger of the Almighty, and know that everything was in order. We were all safe in His hands, always. I wish there was still something to look at which gave me the same feeling. I want, even now, to be safe in His hands.

Yet I had not thought of that banner for years. Leaning in over the sleeping child I must have wanted to see myself as the angel, hovering in protection of an infant who was so obviously in peril.

I turned with burnished wings to face the wicked young mother, accusing words already at the roof of my mouth. I was going to abuse her. I was going to threaten her with the law. I think I even intended to gather up the sleeping bundle in my arms and take it away from this dreadful precipice.

Indignation and righteousness burned in my soul, unquenchably so.

But as I whirled round I saw that she had already taken off most of her clothes.

She stood directly under the fanlight in the middle of the room. Moonlight bathed her, as though by design. It was a theatrical triumph of erotic lighting, sinuously contouring her limbs, sensually flowing upon her in silver caresses, dipping here and there in shaped shadow, shining elsewhere like an extra layer on her already sheening, coffee-coloured skin.

'Do you – do you look after the child?' I asked instead, feebly.

'Oh yes!' she said. The 'yes' was a new and strange word, all vowel, stretching in the air.

'You must take care of it.'

'Oh ye-e-e-es.'

I knew that the angel had flown. Called away. I knew there was no burnished gold at my back, only a burning shaft at my loins. Bring me my arrows of desire. Even as I mocked myself I was stepping towards her. Only once since that evening have I seen a more beautiful woman, a quiet girl sipping coffee in a tawdry dump misnamed The Lollipop. An inaccessible lady.

But this one, standing before me in her underwear, was immediately possessable, if possession means the same thing as physical penetration, or if possession is something you measure by its financial cost, and if possession is acknowledged to be temporary, a leasehold, an object you lose or abandon.

Whenever I take hold of a woman I feel as though my feet are slithering on tufted grass and goat willow. I also expect her to struggle. There is at these times a hot, sweet taste on my tongue, the taste of blood. I am also so excited, so appalled, so outside myself that I can look down at myself, so peculiarly detached, and yet also so vividly held stickily intact within myself that nothing makes sense and the moments do not join together in any comprehensible scale of time. This dislocated alternation of joy and fear, anxiety and compulsion, of being outside and inside, and of time that is distorted away from the normal sequence, is difficult to put into words, later words, linear words: but once, in a friend's flat in Holland Park, I heard the opening passages of a gramophone record which *almost* caught it: Bartok's Sonata for Two Pianos and Percussion. I asked him to play something else and I have never heard it since.

Of course I forgot about the sleeping child. Of course I did.

'Do you want me to keep this on?' she asked me.

'For a minute,' I said. It would not only delay the pleasure, but increase the intensity of it. I always left the dollop of jam in the middle of my mother's puddings until it was the last mouthful.

We went over to the other bed, the higher and wider one. I could see now, in the better light, that a long mirror was on the wall directly over the bed. I would simply have to twist my head during copulation to see what it looked like. It would not be me, nor even an image of me.

'It's only a bloody picture!', a voice from the dead, right on cue.

'Get your clothes off then,' said this living girl as she sat on the bed. I wish she hadn't sounded quite so bored, nor in so much of a hurry. Pornographers always forget those bits.

As I removed my clothes I was glad that the light was so poor. My skin was undoubtedly near to normal in appearance, but a bright light might have exaggerated the slight roughness or the diminishing pinky-red cartography of certain areas on my body. When this happened I used to make up elaborate and probably unconvincing stories about car crashes, burns, skin grafts, incompetent surgeons and so on, anything rather than use the word 'disease'.

These women must get used to all sorts and conditions of men. They don't mind who clambers on top of them. They can lie back, having been paid, and say, in effect, come into me all you who are weary and heavily-laden, all you who are halt and lame, sick and malformed, stunted and twisted, lonely and disturbed. There are plenty around like me. Trade can't be too bad, not for the priest nor for the prostitute. The sacred and the profane are both functions of the same impossible yearning.

Undressed, I lay alongside the one hundred and fifty-sixth of her kind and shuddered as her fingers touched my erect penis. My pleasure-dome.

'Mmmm,' with simulated pleasure, 'this is a nice big one!'

But they always say that. It is part of the ritual, or a prologue to the drama. It works, too. And it works the better as the fingers slide and touch and play while you close your eyes and empty your head of every other sensation being fed into it.

You? No, I should not have moved into the second person.

You do not know about these things. You had no idea what was going on. You would be so shocked and so disgusted that whatever faint chance of your return is left would disappear for ever. You would not have been able to take in the words I had planned to say that night, the night of number one hundred and fifty-six. Would you? Would you?

You? No, I have moved into the wrong sex, too.

The You is you, always you. I can't scrape you off my mind nor even, it seems, off the end of my pen. When I first wrote 'you' a paragraph or so ago I meant it in the general, anonymous sense, universal second person. I am startled to find myself addressing *you* instead.

Think back to that night at the end of September. It was the night the boil finally burst open and the pus of it turned into a reeking torrent that swept us apart. You leapt for the cleaner banks and I allowed myself to be carried on by the filth of deceit, of shame, and of a guilt that even now I cannot put into public or private words. We parted then, you and I, and that is my punishment. There are other pains still to come, for none can hide himself in a secret place where the deeds he has done will not search him out. Do they not fill the earth? Do they not lurk on the surface of every shape, in the resonance of every sound, in the hue of every colour, and at the root of every plant?

Perhaps the worst scourge is the thought that you might have listened and might have understood if I had managed to tell you what had happened.

You brought me a blue card the other week. An appointment at the hospital. Does that mean that you think I am mad? Or does it mean that you have somehow glimpsed the anguish in me, or even guessed at the cause? Does it mean that you still *care*?

But I knocked you to the floor, and the blow was so hard that it made my hand throb for hours afterwards.

I found the card the next morning. My immediate wish was to tear it up. But I have carried it about with me – as I do your photograph, and less worthy things – and I have kept it because it is almost certainly your last message to me. Although it has none of your words on it, nor no other mark of you, I have by slow degrees and probably much self-deception turned it into a love letter from you. I see your tenderness in the bureaucratic print. I transform the detail of time (11.00 a.m.) and place (Brook Green) into gentle words on blue notepaper instead of simple administrative letters or figures on a blue card.

The name of the doctor you want me to see is Pool. Add an 'e' on the end of his name, my love.

Poole. Thomas Poole. Remember?

When I was immersed in my book on Coleridge I used to read you some of his letters. There was one in particular which might have stayed in your mind. I read it to you in bed, a couple of years ago, or maybe longer. But before I got to the end of it I burst into tears. A moment later and I might have straightened myself. I was then, for the first time in our marriage, on the edge of confession. You were extremely puzzled, but also full of concern.

But the moment went by. I got up and made coffee. And, as so often, I did not come back to bed. You did not speak to me next morning, nor for the whole of the next day. We endured in our separate miseries the wilderness of unspoken recrimination, accusation and regret. A wilderness which gradually widened until not a single shrub of hope was left. We ended up in the desert and we did not even see the same mirage.

My mirage shimmered with female limbs and foliated cunt. This was the true shape of my sigh at midnight. I walked in a desert of barren obsession. But if I had called out you would then have heard me across the stones. We could have started again along a happier route, a fertile crescent.

It is too late now.

Pool. Poole. Letter. Card. What does it matter! But I *will* go to see this man. Eleven o'clock, tomorrow morning. It won't do any good but it is the only way that I can reply to your last love letter or apologize for that cruel punch at your face. This Pool who is not Poole cannot be worse than the last idiot I saw from the same backward profession: he was extremely fortunate that I did not send the details of his impertinences to the Medical Association or whatever it is called.

And yet – I am too hasty, too defensive –

Yes, he *did* identify that mirage, or illusions, delusions very close in configuration to it.

I must be more open to the insights of others. I know that I cannot endure alone. I know you will not come back to me. But if, if, I can make myself whole, or be made whole with the help of others, then it is my duty to submit to the pains of healing, the lashes of contempt. I would rather taste ash on my tongue than blood in my mouth.

Shame and penance are not the same things. I want to move out of one and into the other. It is a difficult journey, particularly when one is misled by sudden exultations which seem to offer an almost magical release but so quickly dissipate into even worse depression and remorse. I only have to look back over my own words to see the ups and downs of my own struggle. I appear to have been writing for years, and yet not one sentence has been completed.

Lucy – listen! – I cannot even use my own words to call to you. They shrivel on the page. I cried over that old letter, that fragment of academe, because it said in part what I had wanted, then wanted and still want to say to you and only to you, and because it expressed in part some of the physical ache and fear and disappointment I had felt, then felt and still (in an increased measure) feel.

When I used to read to you in bed you must have thought that Coleridge's mummified corpse was lying between us. You fell asleep once when I went droning on through *Biographia Literaria*. I kept it up until I was certain you were not hearing a word. Your breathing was deep and regular, you were surely asleep, out of the world. Without any apparent break in the text and without any change of tone in my voice I got out some of the things I so badly needed to tell you. It was part confession, part explanation, but mostly a plea. I had a terrible shock when you opened your eyes and looked so steadily at me.

Had you heard?

I carried on at the same point in the book and you did not seem to notice. But you touched me on the cheek. 'A debility and dimness of the imaginative power,' I read, in panic, 'and a consequent necessity of reliance on the immediate impressions of the senses, do, we well know, render the mind liable to superstition and fanaticism——'

'Oh, for Christ's sake,' you complained, not urgently.

Drowsy, you wanted to make love. And, yet again, I could not manage it.

'Christ Almighty!' you complained. Bitterly.

There had been long periods when I could only enter you and come in you by secretly pretending to myself that I did not know you, that you were a tart I had picked up in a bar or on the street corner. You had to be part of my mirage.

But when you were My Princess I could not bear to imagine you stained by me. I did not and could not touch you where you wanted to be touched. It made me feel sick.

Oh, those moments after we had made love. The gloom that fell upon me was deep enough to make me want to die. I cannot, cannot, cannot explain it, cannot understand it.

Pool. Poole. What's the odds!

There were moments when I all but spoke the truth. But that night at the end of September which ended in revulsion and hatred so far as you were concerned had earlier come to a much more disgusting climax. I use this last word with awful irony. Word?

'Mmm' the Guyanese voice says, 'this is a nice big one!'

Singing in the Rain. My Blue Heaven. I've Got A Date With An Angel. The Very Thought of You. You Are My Lucky Star. Smoke Gets In Your Eyes. You Are My Sunshine. Moonstruck. Stardust.

Tea For Two. All things Bright and Beautiful.

An Old Fashioned Tan-go. All creatures Big and Small.

Deep Purple. Deepening purple. Smoky voice coming up the stair.

A child calling out, on his hands and knees. A child leaning over the edge of a precipice. A child turning from the tree. A child in a world where the Angel had gone.

You May Not Be An Angel. All things Wise and Wonderful.

Foxtrot. Foxglove. Fox eye. The Lord God Made Them All.

Let me sing to you, then. No, let me read to you. Lie back and – no, no, listen. Listen.

'In the education of children, love is first to be instilled, and out of

love obedience is to be educed.' No, don't touch me. Not there. Please! '*Then impulse and power should be given to the intellect, and the ends of a moral being be exhibited. For this object thus much is effected by works of imagination; – that they carry the mind out of self, and show the possible of the good and the great in the human character. The height, whatever it may be, of the imaginative standard will do no harm; we are commanded to imitate one who is inimitable.*' Turn to meet Him and he will break your arm. Thumb in mouth.

Children with thumbs in their mouths. Whores with cocks in their mouths. Rustling tree, slithering nylon. Deep Purple. God walking up and down between buckthorn and sallow and goat willow.

'*We should address ourselves to those faculties in a child's mind, which are first awakened by nature, and consequently first admit of cultivation, that is to say, the memory and the imagination.*' Good boy, good boy, good boy.

Throw it in the bin! The bin!

And baby makes three . . .

'*The comparing power, the judgement, is not at that age active, and ought not to be forcibly excited——*' You don't like this? But it's a good piece, and – you think I'll never write the book, don't you? You think everything has gone wrong just because I won't won't won't fuck you.

Don't you *like* Coleridge? Let me go on a bit. Listen a while longer. Please. I've been making notes on it, all evening. When you were at the cinema.

'I didn't go to the cinema,' you said. 'I didn't go last week either, nor the week before, nor the week before that. I was somewhere else.'

'*The imagination is the distinguishing——*'

'I didn't go to the cinema!'

My Princess. Listen. 'The imagination is the distinguishing characteristic of man as a progressive being; and I repeat that it ought to be carefully guided and strengthened as the indispensable means and instrument of continued amelioration and refinement.' *Why are you crying? Why don't you listen?* 'Men of genius and goodness are generally restless in their minds in the present, and this, because they are by a law of their nature unremittingly regarding themselves in the future, and contemplating the possible of moral and intellectual advance towards perfection.' *Oh, shut up! Listen!* 'Thus we live by hope and faith, thus we are for the most part able to realize what we will, and thus we accomplish the end of our being. The contemplation of futurity inspires humility of soul in our judgement of the present.'

I even tried to read to you that night at the end of last September. Why did I choose the same piece, The Education of Children?

You wouldn't have it, wouldn't listen. You said I was *sick*.

Three hours earlier a lilting voice had told me that I had a nice big cock. She had enough honour in her to be mindful of the considerable fee. She put her mouth over it, licking, sucking, dribbling, both of us unaware by now of the child sleeping three or four paces across the half-dark room. Her fingers stroked my balls and her lips slid on my penis and in a few minutes, free to call her what I wished, I pulled her down and mounted her.

And then I want my shaft to be as long as a furlong and time to stand still and my tongue to be dipped in honey.

'Dirty rotten fucker, dirty cunt!' I say, not yet exploding with pleasure.

'Yes!' she says, picking up the signal. 'I'm a dirty cunt. Juicy cunt.'

Head twisting to look in the dark glass above the creaking bed. Body push, push, pushing. Words spurting. Goat willow crushing. Oak tree hard. Blue hills in the mirror. Black mountains on the headboard.

Delay. Delay. Delay.

'I'll – come – in – your – mouth – after – !'

'Ye-e-es. Dirty fucker. Dirty boy.'

Delay it. Delay.

'Slimy bitch. Filthy whore. Slippery cunt.'

'Ye-e-es!'

Delay. Delay. Delay. Start counting as the juices come up to the boil. Rings on the grass. Labels on the bottle. Trees by the path. Pig on a bench. Start counting. Sheep in the shelter, count them.

One two three four five six *not yet* seven eight nine *no no* ten eleven twelve *wait* thirteen fourteen *no!* fifteen *not yet!* sixteen *wait, wait, wait* seventeen *wait!* seventeen seventeen eighteen *no use* nineteen the stuff was *Co-ming!* twent——

I must have shouted out at that precise moment where exultation turns to disgust, the moment of spilling, of defilement.

A shout loud enough to wake the child. The child began to scream. I thought at first that the sound, the terrorized shriek, was my last spurt, expressing itself.

Did you expect me to tell you *that*? Lucy? You, who wanted me to enter you on the same night, with the same sound still in my head, a sound that I knew I had somehow, somewhere, heard before.

You said I was *sick*. It was you that was sick, wanting to do such a thing. I am better off without you.

And you know what you can do with your blue card, you cunning little bitch. You don't even begin to measure up against that gentle creature in The Lollipop. *She* would listen to me reading Coleridge, black hair falling over her sweet face, red boots at the side of the bed.

PART SIX

TRYING TO BEGIN

He tore the pages up into big pieces and then he tore the big pieces up into tiny pieces. It was already afternoon, and it was still freezing outside. He had not washed. He had not shaved. He had not eaten. His head was buzzing once more like a summer forest, and the blue appointment card was still in his pocket. He had yet again prevented himself from destroying it.

His hands now were lustrous with silvery scales flaking off ugly patches of red. The fingers, coiling in towards the palm, were scarcely capable of holding the pen. Blood trickled down his calves where, while writing, he had clawed at the cracking patches on his legs.

This was not endurable.

He took out his wallet, hoping to find something hidden within the pigskin.

A photograph of a fair girl with green eyes. He studied it, then kissed it. A yellowed cutting about an old murder. He did not need to read it. Library ticket. Driving Licence. Blue card. Advertisement for a cottage in the Forest of Dean. . . .

He was fairly sure that he remembered the cottage, nearly

three miles along a track into the woods, close by an abandoned quarry and a little further from a small coalmine once worked by four of his distant cousins. The mine had its tunnel driven into the side of a steep bank, making the hill look as though it had a toothless mouth. Four or five hundred yards from the black hole the trees on the slope had sagged towards each other, disturbed by the human moles working beneath their long roots.

But –

But, yes, he had written this. Weeks ago.

Moreover, he had written it on pages that he could not at this moment tear up into big pieces and then into smaller pieces. They were the pages on his agent's desk. The giveaway. The exposing sheets, probably already being duplicated or pawed over.

Thank God he had destroyed the rest!

He considered, now, that he should have spent the time he had wasted on *all that fiction* in working on his great book on Samuel Taylor Coleridge instead. He remembered the excitements which had preceded the disaster: the origins of Kubla Khan, the crystal and the ice, the dome and the pleasure-dome, the genii and the dreams.

Novels were far inferior in structure and content to these triumphs.

He put the things back into his wallet, except for the blue card informing him that he was to see Dr Pool in the morning. He examined the card, and began to laugh.

Pool. Poole.

Those poems and letters and essays were *real*. He should address himself to them, these graces from the past. It was the contemplation of what had been which inspired humility of soul in our judgement of the present. Coleridge had to be corrected on this point. But, then, he could not have foreseen such terrible days as these, when 'the contemplation of futurity' inspired only fear and dread.

He twisted the appointment card in his hands.

Coleridge had this optimism, whatever bodily pain that letter to Poole showed he suffered, because, because – ?

Because he believed in God!

That same essay – The Education of Children – was calm in this belief. He raked back through pages in his mind. He was reading again to his wife, poor bored Lucy.

'I think the memory of children cannot, in reason, be too much stored with the objects and facts of natural history. God opens the images of nature, like the leaves of a book, before the eyes of his creature, Man – and teaches him all that is grand and beautiful in the foaming cataract, the glassy lake, and the floating mist.'

Shepherd's Bush yielded up none of these things, unless you counted carbon monoxide as a floating mist and the people coming out of the underground station as a foaming cataract.

It was no place for a man to live. How was it possible to finish his book in the midst of such concreted and asphalted blasphemies?

His mind swung back to the Forest he had left so many years before. He had made Daniel Miller run for cover into those remembered trees. He had left him asleep in the cottage, an act of mercy. The car, presumably, was still parked outside.

The blue card revolved in his hands.

Through the window the wind was making noises in the stripped trees. But he knew that this was not actually so, not really the case. Better, though, if it could be. Better to be his own character.

He could make Miller wake up now. He could heal Miller's skin. Give him money. Take the pain out of his joints. Finish his, Miller's, book on Coleridge. Bring back his wife. He could do anything with, to or for this fictional character, simply by lifting up his pen.

The car, presumably, was still parked outside?

He put the card face down on the table and brushed off the

torn fragments of paper with the side of his sore hand. Begin again.

The car – he thought – is still parked outside, the rain drumming on its roof, the iced mud packed round the wheels. But it is day now, there in the Forest. He could make it warmer if he wanted to. He could put green back on the trees, blue back into the sky, purple into the undergrowth. Why not? What were novels *for*?

He was the narrator. The Author. Creator of all!

The narrator of a novel can do anything, with the people, the things, the machines, the landscape, the lot. Can any hide in his pages that he shall not see him? Does not he fill in every word from cover to cover?

Do not I fill heaven and earth, if heaven and earth are words on my page?

He picked up the blue card again, thinking about his novel. He crossed out the name Pool.

'It is, of course, no accident,' he said out loud, testing to see if the words would come out on a printed page in a bound volume, 'that redundant theological speculation about the death of God should run parallel with an equally tedious literary preoccupation with the death of the novel.'

He waited; patient, alert, ready to take the only way now that he could escape to the Forest of Dean.

It is, of course, no accident that redundant theological speculation about the death of God should run parallel with an equally tedious literary preoccupation with the death of the novel.

The thrill was stupendous. He moved his finger along the line, just here. This was better than the label on the bottle of Camp coffee. There was more detail. He wrote in the name *Hadley*, on the card.

Where did it start and where did it end? Or does it go on and on and on and on?

He cleared his head of false sensation and searched for the beginning. A clock went tick-h, tock-h, tick-h, tock-h, then stopped, abruptly. He decided to get back between the covers, or under the covers.

The beginning! It came up at him like a smack across the chops from a hand wet with soapy water. Here it was: and starting here he was both fucking *and* getting back into the tree.

One two three four five six *not yet* seven eight nine *no, no* ten eleven twelve *wait* thirteen fourteen *no!* fifteen *not yet!* sixteen *wait, wait, wait* seventeen *wait!* seventeen seventeen eighteen *no use* nineteen the words (the stuff) were *Co-ming!* twent——

'He knows I am trying to escape,' I announced, abruptly, glad to be here again.

'Who does? *Who* knows?'

'The Author.' Yes, I was working it out.

The two fresh-faced medical students sitting on the big table stopped swinging their legs. Dr Hadley, who had asked the questions, ceased to play with the two-toned ball pen he had been using as a remote muscle of his tongue. A medicine trolley squeaked rodently in the hall outside, where other out-patients sat in clumps of tubular steel chairs neatly arranged according to their various diseases. I abandoned the effort to count up to a hundred, sensing that brightly coloured biochemicals were jiggling together on the page. Let bards sing now of barbiturates as bright as violets.

'What author?' asked the doctor, probably resenting the arbitrary change that had been made upon his name. Uptight idiot.

I sighed. I have, after all, attempted to answer this before, if to no avail.

'The Author of this Book,' I replied, twisting my head away a little, pretending shame.

The two silent students looked at each other, eyebrows arching. It was just as I had arranged, word for word.

'Which book are you talking about, Mr Coleridge?' persisted Dr Hadley, expressionless. Oh, I'm no fool. I remember the sequence well, the bit immediately after 'all that is grand and beautiful in the foaming cataract, the glassy lake, and the floating mist'.

THE COMMON MODERN NOVEL, IN WHICH THERE IS NO IMAGINATION, BUT A MISERABLE STRUGGLE TO EXCITE AND GRATIFY MERE CURIOSITY, OUGHT, IN MY JUDGEMENT, TO BE WHOLLY FORBIDDEN TO CHILDREN. NOVEL-READING OF THIS SORT IS ESPECIALLY INJURI-OUS TO THE GROWTH OF THE IMAGINATION, THE JUDGEMENT, AND THE MORALS, ESPECIALLY TO THE LATTER, BECAUSE IT EXCITES MERE FEELINGS WITHOUT AT THE SAME TIME MINIS-TERING AN IMPULSE TO ACTION.

I didn't answer his question, not immediately. This was a new intrusion, the capitals.

'These things ought, in my judgement, to be wholly for-bidden to children,' I said, instead.

'What things?'

'Sexual assault.'

Predictably, there was a pause. Three faces lit up, beaming in upon what they thought was a crucial fact. They looked extremely silly, trying not to slaver, munching on their own teeth.

'You look extremely silly in this Book, you know,' I said, a little unkindly.

'Which book are you talking about,' persisted Hadley or Pool or whoever.

'*This* Book. The Book I am in. And so the Book you are in. And the Book those two men swinging their legs over there are in.'

Now that I had got it out I leaned back in my tubular steel chair with just the suggestion of a smirk on my face. Only half convinced of the truth of my new thesis, and not wholly sure of where exactly I am, I can nevertheless recognize with some satisfaction that perhaps the most disconcerting thing a character in a novel can do is to announce that he is indeed a character in a novel.

As I reach the open air on the far side of the back cover, having emerged from a cavern called the dungeon of lust, ten thousand voices will greet me with a joyous shout.

'Long live our hero, whom the mountains of Tasgi have brought forth!'

But since I am not real and they are not real you might as well stop reading at about this point. Go back to Part Three, which was supposed to provide the original ending. My hand aches. My real hand does, too. I am, in the mid-course of my life, looking for the straight path through the trees.